HIS LOVELY VIRGIN

A BILLIONAIRE FIRST LOVE ROMANCE

HAPPILY EVER BILLIONAIRES
BOOK FOUR

VIVIAN WOOD

AUTHOR'S COPYRIGHT

HIS VIRGIN

1

Meredith Fields frowned while looking at her reflection in the antique full-length mirror. She looked like a stripper in the skimpy cobalt blue sequined dress she was wearing. Her breasts were dangerously close to being fully exposed, and the hem barely covered her butt. A daring cutout across her stomach displayed even more skin, and to top it all off, the dress was backless.

Ugh, she groaned silently.

She wasn't a fan of wearing revealing outfits. Plus, the heavy makeup she had applied made her feel even more self-conscious. But she'd wanted to go all out for the vintage-themed party she was attending that evening with her best friend, Lily Waldorf.

After all, many high-profile people would certainly be in attendance. Thanks to Lily's well-connected family, they would be partying with politicians, actors, and models tonight.

"Oh, come on! You look hot," Lily said reassuringly after seeing Meredith scowling at herself in the mirror. She stood next to her, wearing a silver version of Meredith's dress, putting on a pair of glittery hoop earrings.

"I know," Meredith responded confidently, then twirled on her heels and checked her reflection once more.

She had to admit, she was looking pretty good. The rich jewel tone blue of the dress really complemented her complexion.

"Are you sure you're not coming to Bali?" Lily asked as she checked her makeup one last time in the mirror.

Meredith's face fell at the reminder that she would be spending her entire summer back in Washington, D.C. She'd just completed her degree in journalism from Columbia University, and was supposed to be spending the rest of the year enjoying a well-deserved vacation. But her father had made her a very tempting offer – come back to D.C. and work for him over the summer, and he would release her trust fund early.

It had hardly been a choice at all. She could spend several years partying with that amount of money. And she figured two months would pass before she knew it.

"Yeah, I'm sure. As much as I really want to go with you, this is the first time my dad's made me an offer like this. So I think I should take him up on this before he changes his mind," Meredith replied while rolling her eyes.

She didn't expect him to cancel the deal on her, but she supposed anything was possible. After all, she'd never imagined he would have budged an inch when it came to her trust fund. She wasn't supposed to see a penny of that money until she was thirty, but that seemed so far away. Plus, Meredith figured she'd be married with kids by then, and her carefree days of partying and drinking would be long behind her.

"Your dad's a pretty wise person," Lily commented with a chuckle.

"He is," Meredith responded after applying another layer of blood-red lipstick. "And he really knows how to push my buttons," she muttered under her breath.

Yep, Benedict Percival Fields was the shrewdest person Meredith had ever known. He owned the largest newspaper company in the country. Meredith had learned the ins and outs of the industry from an early age, but she'd still wanted to earn a degree in journalism. That way no one could say she wasn't qualified to work at her father's company.

She just didn't want to waste the best years of her life slaving away at a desk job. Going straight from university to the workforce wasn't exactly how she had envisioned life after graduation. Thoughts of Bali and an easygoing summer spent partying in the sand had given her life during her final exams.

But she didn't have a choice, did she?

"So, what's this deal of his entail?" Lily asked.

Meredith shrugged, still checking out their reflections. The two of them would surely stand out tonight in their outfits, but somehow she was starting to feel less self-conscious. The dress emphasized her curves just as much as it showed some skin, and she knew she looked good. The nervousness she felt was starting to give way to excitement.

"I don't know the details. We haven't talked about it yet," she answered.

Meredith moved to take a seat on the bed and stared admiringly at Lily's waist-length, fiery red hair. Lily's tanned skin looked stunning in her silver dress. She could tell that Lily was excited for tonight's event as well.

It figured. Lily was the number one partygoer she had ever met.

"Enough about me. What about you? How are things going with your family?" Meredith asked, carefully strapping on a pair of black high heels.

Lily's expression immediately turned sour. Meredith knew she never liked to think about family matters. It wasn't because she didn't care about them. It was just because she almost never saw either of her parents.

They were too busy to even remember she existed.

And that was probably a big part of why Meredith and Lily had hit it off so well after meeting at freshman orientation. Meredith often lamented over how overbearing her parents could be. On the other hand, Lily was desperate for her parents' attention.

"Still the same as ever," Lily responded, rolling her eyes and sighing before sitting next to Meredith on the bed. "I told them I'm going straight to Europe after my Bali trip and the only response I got was, 'Okay honey, have fun.'"

"That's it?" Meredith's eyes widened reflexively, although she wasn't surprised. In truth, she felt envious. She'd often wondered how nice it would be to have the freedom to do whatever she wanted without the fear of disappointing her parents.

"Yeah. It makes me sick."

"Aren't you happy? I mean, at least you get to do whatever you want."

"I don't know. Of course Bali and Europe are going to be fun. But I still don't know what I want to do with my life, unlike you. You've got things all figured out. And I know you think your parents are pushy, but at least your dad cares enough about you to push you," Lily murmured with a sad smile on her lips.

Silence filled the room.

Meredith didn't know what to say. Because at moments like this, it was Lily who made her see just how lucky she was to have parents like hers. And deep down, she knew Lily was right. Her father was just helping her out, trying to show her the right path to achieve her goals in life.

But don't you think you've earned the right to enjoy a few months off after all these years of hitting the books? a voice whispered at the back of her mind.

Shrugging off the idea, Meredith glanced at Lily, who was back in front of the mirror again, styling her hair. She seemed to be deciding between wearing it in a high pony-tail or leaving it down. Either way, she would still look hot.

"Anyway, this is the last party we'll be attending together for the next couple of months. Let's make the most out of it. I didn't call in every favor I had to get us on the VIP list for this party just to be all doom and gloom tonight," Lily said, breaking the awkward silence.

A mischievous smile appeared on Lily's face as she turned to face her. Meredith was more than aware of where the conversation was headed, and she was dreading it.

"Who knows? Tonight might be the night you finally lose your V-card, Mer," Lily squealed in excitement.

"Hey! Don't say that," Meredith protested quietly, bowing her head as she felt her cheeks grow hot. Yep, she was already twenty-three but still a virgin. And she was proud of it.

"Oh, come on," Lily groaned, stomping her foot like a kid about to throw a temper tantrum.

"I'm not a prude, and you know that, Lily! I'm just... saving it for someone special," she said defensively, staring at the floor.

Meredith may have been born and raised in the city, but she'd always believed giving up her virginity was something to be taken seriously. She wanted it to be with someone who would make her feel breathless – someone extraordinary.Just like in the movies, she wanted it to be magical.

Lily snorted. "I know. I've seen all those romance books you read." She shook her head, but then her expression softened.

"You've got some catching up to do, but your first time is going to be special. And tonight? Tonight is definitely special."

Feeling amused at the 180-degree turn of their conversation, Meredith raised her head and smiled at her best friend. Lily was right. Tonight was going to be special. It was the first party they'd be attending after graduating from college, and they were ready to make the most of it.

"Whatever," she murmured, trying to downplay the excitement that had started to engulf her. Deep down, she couldn't deny she was hoping things would turn out to be magical.

But she had a feeling this night was going to end up bad.

2

Meredith took a deep breath before exiting the limo, following Lily's lead. They'd arrived at a luxurious mansion in the middle of the city. She was used to the party scene, but for some reason she was feeling more anxious than excited. She'd had ample time to think during the ride over, and she couldn't stop imagining any number of worst-case scenarios.

Relax. It's not like anything bad's going to happen, she quietly reassured herself, then did a series of breathing exercises to calm her nerves.

"Relax," Lily muttered as if reading her mind, then slipped a silver silk mask adorned with crystals into place. She gave Meredith a light nudge, urging her to put on her mask, too.

"Do we really have to?" she asked, suddenly feeling unsure and reluctant.

Masks weren't exactly the first accessories she'd have picked out. But part of her found the idea appealing. Concealing their identities meant they could dance and drink with abandon, hiding behind the guise of anonymity.

"Yep. I told you, some very famous people are here. No one's allowed in without a mask, and that's pretty much the only rule for tonight."

She rolled her eyes, but Meredith obliged and followed suit. The mask covered more than half of her face. She startled slightly when she saw a masked usher approaching them, but then she realized the mask rule applied to the staff as well. *They're really taking this whole anonymity angle seriously*, she thought.

"Good evening, ladies. Your names, please?" said the usher after taking a small, polite bow. He stood expectantly, holding a clipboard to his chest.

"Lily. Lily Waldorf," her best friend said taking the lead, gripping her wrist to emphasize they were together. "And Meredith Fields."

After a few moments of scanning the names on his clipboard, the man nodded and smiled at them. Despite his mask, Meredith could tell he was attractive, making her feel less anxious and decidedly more excited about what the night had in store for them.

It's going to be an interesting night, she thought with a smile on her lips.

"This way please," the man spoke in a louder voice as they stepped into the mansion.

Booming music reverberated throughout the halls, and the air smelled like booze. Looking around, Meredith saw people getting into cozy booths lined up like tiny turtles. As she stole a glance at a couple on her right, she caught a glimpse of both a tiny couch and bed within the plush enclosure.

The center of the large ballroom was packed with sweaty bodies gyrating to the heavy thumping bass of the music. She blushed when she realized most of the women were wearing much less than her and Lily. Some were even wearing what appeared to be nothing more than strategically placed strips of leather and latex, and she tried desperately not to stare.

Be happy you're in a dress.

A masked waiter passed them by, and Meredith was more than happy to quickly down a shot of tequila. A little liquid courage couldn't hurt, right? She turned to ask Lily if she wanted a shot, but her friend was nowhere to be found. Looking around, she slowly realized Lily was already dancing with a masked stranger, looking for all the world like she was having the time of her life.

Damn Lily.

"Hey!" Lily called out, waving at her as if she'd only just now remembered they'd come to the party together.

Meredith pointed at herself with a wry grin before shaking her head. Dancing while sober was something she had never done in her entire life. She wasn't up for a dance – not yet. Maybe after a few more shots she'd be ready.

She staked out a seat at the bar, content to sit and just observe her surroundings for the moment. Her eyes never left Lily's figure as she gulped down shot after shot of vodka.

Damn, girl. You know how to drink, she thought, praising herself.

When the alcohol finally hit her, Meredith was more than ready to party. She rose from her seat and grinned when a tall blond guy made eye contact with her and took her hand in his, pulling her toward the dance floor.

"I'm Luke," the blond guy introduced himself, resting both of his hands on her waist before they moved to her back, caressing her skin.

"Meredith," she said, moving closer to him and dancing seductively, pressing her body to his. "It's nice to meet you, Meredith," he whispered huskily.

Meredith moaned when she felt his hand slip under the hem of her dress. She knew he was crossing the line when he touched her bare ass, but she loved what he was doing. The shots had made her bold.

"It's nice to meet you, too," she murmured as she rubbed against him.

Pulling Luke even closer, she caressed his hard chest, enjoying the feel of his strong muscles underneath her hands. She felt like she was close to shedding her inhibitions, but in a good kind of way.

Just when she was about to suggest moving to a booth to continue their fun in private, Luke was pulled away by another stranger. A woman wearing a red leather corset, black satin thong and black fishnets shoved him down onto the nearest chair before straddling him and giving him the bitchiest lap dance she had ever seen, glaring at Meredith when their eyes met. Luke, on the other hand, looked more than happy to be in his current position.

I should have known he was taken, she thought glumly as she marched back to her seat from earlier at the bar.

Her eyes roamed over the crowd as she searched for Lily, but she couldn't find her. Her best friend was probably already having the time of her life. *At least one of us is*, she thought.

Just then, Meredith realized that over half of the females in attendance were wearing nothing but lingerie.

"Unbelievable, right?" the female bartender said after noticing Meredith's obvious staring. She poured her another shot of vodka without prompting. Like everyone else, she was wearing a mask.

"Are they hired performers? Or are they guests?" Meredith asked, genuinely curious.

"Everyone here except for the staff and security are guests," the bartender answered with a knowing smile. Meredith could tell the woman knew exactly what she was thinking.

"So these women are basically taking advantage of the masquerade to hook up," she said haltingly, since she'd just pieced everything together. She remembered the furnishings she'd noticed earlier in the booth, and blushed.

"You bet."

She tipped her shot back, wincing as the vodka burned her throat on the way down, warming her chest. She looked back at the writhing throng of people on the dance floor. These women were from prominent, wealthy families, just like her.

Her gaze came to rest on Luke, who was now making out with the woman from earlier. She grimaced when she saw the woman openly caressing the evident bulge in Luke's slacks.

Fuckers.

"I did not bring you here to watch couples making out," said a familiar voice at her side. She swiveled around to find Lily, looking like she'd just come down from heaven.

Maybe she really had.

"Where were you?" Meredith asked, looking closely at her best friend's face.

"Somewhere over there – having a little taste of heaven." Lily had a sly smirk on her face.

Rolling her eyes, Meredith examined Lily carefully. If she was already trashed, it was going to be a real buzzkill. Lily glared at her.

"Mer, will you just relax and enjoy yourself already? What's so wrong about kissing a few guys and having some fun? Besides, you're wearing a mask. You could finally have sex without anyone even knowing who you are," Lily said matter-of-factly.

"I was enjoying myself. But someone stole my guy from me," she retorted, crossing her arms across her chest as she remembered how easily Luke had been whisked away.

"So steal him back. Whoever she was, I know she's got nothing on you. Be confident. And follow me," Lily said with a wink. She downed a shot of tequila before taking Meredith by the wrist.

Meredith found herself being dragged into the crowd once more, dancing with Lily like there was no tomorrow. Her best friend was right. There was nothing to worry about. All she needed to do was let loose.

Tonight, she could be the most carefree version of herself.

3

———

$\mathcal{E}$lijah and Jack stretched as they exited Henry's car, parked several yards away from the mansion. As per usual, they were attempting to keep a low profile in order to avoid the prying eyes of the media. This was their first night out in ages.

Having worked nonstop for months now gearing up for his presidential campaign, Elijah Scott finally had a couple of hours to spare to catch up with his friends. And by catching up, he meant partying and letting loose like the bachelor he was. He didn't intend to waste a single second.

It's going to be a wild night, he thought.

"Hey, don't forget your masks," Henry called out from the driver's seat while checking his reflection in the rearview mirror.

Right, the only real rule about tonight's party was that everyone had to wear a mask. And truthfully it was the only reason he was even able to attend.

Tonight, he was free to party without being judged.

And he could be as bad as he wanted.

"I never thought I'd be asked to hide my good looks under some ridiculous mask in order to attend a party," Jack joked sarcastically, a smirk spreading across his handsome features.

"Fuck off, Jack," Henry said amicably, with no real heat in his voice. "Guess you'll just have to rely on your winning personality for a change," he quipped as Jack chuckled.

Ever flirtatious and charming, women loved his friends. But Eli also knew the idea of hiding who they were was more than a little foreign to them. Shrugging at the hilarity of the situation, Elijah put on his mask.

He didn't have a choice, did he?

Concealing his true identity was the only way he'd be able to attend a party like this one. His opponents would stop at nothing to discredit him, and if the media knew about this, he'd never be elected. But he couldn't help wanting to enjoy just one night with his friends. It had been so long.

Walking toward the glamorous mansion, Elijah couldn't help but feel a rush of excitement. He couldn't remember the last time he'd been at a wild party – the days had all started to blend together once he'd decided to run for office.

"Hey, are you still going out with Jessica?" he heard Henry ask Jack as they got closer to the entrance. "You'll have to be more specific," Jack replied smugly.

"Just how many Jessicas are you dating?" Elijah asked, shaking his head and giving Jack a playful grin.

"No, Jessica Garner," Henry stated in between frustrated groans. He was obviously interested in her, which was unusual. The women Jack tended to date weren't often Henry's type.

This Jessica must be different, Eli thought.

He laughed as his friends exchanged a confused glance. God, how much he envied them for being able to date around so freely.

So why don't you date someone then? It's not like dating is prohibited for politicians, said a voice in his head.

Dating and marrying had always been part of his plans. But as the only single presidential candidate, he was subjected to intense scrutiny of his personal life, something his opponents didn't have to worry about. And jeopardizing his high approval ratings was something he couldn't do. He needed to remain single, and he needed to be discreet.

"Good evening, gentlemen," greeted a masked usher standing at the entrance of the lavish mansion. They nodded as Henry stepped forward.

"Austin," Henry said quietly, then inclined his head toward Elijah and Jack. "And Dallas and Houston." Elijah half expected the usher to smirk at the obvious fake names Henry had given him, but he just smiled politely and nodded as he scanned through the list on his clipboard. Elijah couldn't leave any kind of paper trail behind tonight, and he'd been counting on Henry to make the proper arrangements. Henry, ever reliable, had come through no problem.

The usher quickly led them to a grand ballroom that looked to already be at capacity. Studying the crowd for a moment, Elijah released a deep breath he didn't realize he'd been holding.

This was exactly what he'd expected.

This is just what I need, he thought.

Even though it had been awhile, he was no stranger to the party scene. But this was something else entirely. The crowd was filled with people who formed the upper echelon of society. Which made it all the more scandalous that all the women in attendance seemed to have forgotten to get dressed for the occasion, save their sexiest lingerie.

Though he wasn't hard yet, he had no doubt he would be soon. And he was free to hook up with no strings attached, and no one being the wiser about who he really was.

"Looks like we've got our pick tonight, eh boys?" Jack said with a wink as they hit the bar.

"Cheers," he said, toasting his friends before they knocked back their shots. He signaled to the female bartender for another round before directing his attention back to his friends.

"You sure you remember how to do this?" Henry asked suddenly. Elijah blinked, momentarily startled, then glared as Henry and Jack began to laugh. Before he could come up with a snappy retort, Henry piped up.

"You've been working your ass off ever since we graduated. Hell, even way before that. As long as we've known you, you've always been a workaholic," he said. Jack snorted.

"What Henry's trying to say is that we're worried your dick doesn't work anymore," he crudely added.

"What the – Are you being serious right now?" Elijah exclaimed incredulously. Sure, maybe he hadn't gone out with them in ages, but it wasn't because he hadn't wanted to.

It's just that fun was a luxury for someone like him.

"Dude, relax. Drink up and enjoy yourself. Once you win the election, you're never going to be able to do this kind of thing again," Jack said, chuckling as he handed him another shot of vodka.

They hit the dance floor, moving in time with the music until they found a slightly less crowded area.

Looking around, Eli saw Jack dancing with a redhead only a couple of feet away. She wore a glittering silver dress which was conservative compared to what most of the other women were wearing, but would still be considered risqué anywhere else.

He always appreciated a good tease.

Jack was clearly doing just fine, mask or not. Elijah looked for Henry next. He found him quickly getting intimately acquainted with a woman wearing a sheer ivory teddy with. Yep, the masks hadn't adversely affected their ability to pick up women one bit. He grinned.

This place was crazy. And he loved it!

It wasn't long before he found himself going with the flow, dancing with a group of women who looked like they were celebrating a bachelorette party. One woman even kissed him, but he soon found himself eyeing a petite blonde across the room. He noted she was wearing the same dress as the redhead from earlier, but in a shade of blue that looked beautiful on her.

He excused himself from the bachelorette party, smiling apologetically when the women pouted. He couldn't keep his eyes off the hot and sexy blonde. Instantly he was hard. He headed toward her, and as he passed Jack and the redhead, she grabbed him by the wrist and pulled them both toward the mystery blonde. He ended up in one of the private booths alone with her before he knew it.

He looked around for his friends, a tiny part of him feeling like he'd been set up. But they were nowhere to be seen.

They're probably enjoying their own private shows, he thought as the blonde slammed him down into a chair and started dancing sexily in front of him.

The music could still be faintly heard within the booth, but it was rapidly drowned out by the sexy sounds coming from the woman who was currently giving him the hottest lap dance he'd ever had in his entire life. She was so bold, rubbing her breasts against him and moaning, and he loved every second of what she was doing.

She straddled him, wrapping her arms around his neck, and pressing her breasts against him. It was taking everything he had not to just grab her and kiss her passionately.She was so fucking sexy. And he wanted desperately to be inside her.

Immediately.

But he couldn't.

A presidential candidate like him knew better. And a random hookup should have been totally out of the question.

He knew all this, yet his self-control was rapidly disappearing. Suddenly she pulled him close for a kiss. Her lips were soft and inviting, and when he felt her playfully nip at his bottom lip, he couldn't help but respond in turn.

Flirting with his hands and mouth was the best he could do, so he decided to make the most of it. He was shocked when she suddenly removed her mask, pulling his head into her cleavage.

"Mmm," she moaned as he started licking her sweaty skin.

Jesus! She tastes so fucking good, he thought, unable to suppress the urge to get a little taste of heaven.

"You taste so fucking good, babe," he said, slightly raising his head to try and see her face. But she kept his head pressed down against her breasts.

"Make me feel good," she murmured in between moans as she rubbed against his crotch.

Eli continued to nibble on her, moving from her neck to her breasts, and back again. He couldn't believe how good she was making him feel. She was driving him insane, and she wasn't even stripping yet!

Lifting his head, he studied her face. She had deep set blue eyes, and full, pouty lips. Her high nose had a thin bridge that matched the rest of her delicate, petite features.

She was easily one of the most beautiful women he had ever seen.

He realized his pulse was pounding. This definitely wasn't normal for him.

He'd met and dated plenty of women in the past. But none of them had affected him like this, and certainly not within such a short time span. Sure, they'd all gorgeous, but his heart racing like this was certainly a first.

Was it because he hadn't hooked up with someone in awhile? He didn't know.

But the one thing Eli did know, was that this woman was not only young, but also drunk. Getting involved with her right now was the last thing he needed to be doing.

"Good girls should be in bed, babe," he whispered.

What little self-control he had left was rapidly eroding, but he was afraid if he made a move now he wouldn't stop until things were too late.

She gave a soft chuckle in his ear. She was alternating between nipping and sucking at his earlobe, and he groaned when he felt her hot breath on his neck.

"Is that an invitation?" she asked sensuously, making his cock pulse with need. Her lips felt so fucking soft, and he wanted to taste and feel more of her.

You're wearing a mask. She'll never know who you are. Eli heard a voice in his head, urging him to give in already.

Right. He was there to have fun. Why was he fighting this? He could tell that she wanted him.

It was mutual.

It didn't have to be as complicated as he was making it, right? They'd hook up, no strings attached, and go their separate ways.

There was nothing wrong with it.

"The bed is here for a reason," Eli spoke huskily, having finally decided to let his monster take over.

"Oh," she said, then giggled. Rising from his lap, she swayed unsteadily on her feet. He was quick to grab her by the waist and keep her from falling over.

Growing impatient, Eli stood up, preparing to scoop her tiny body into his arms and just carry her to the bed. But he'd scarcely entertained the thought when the redhead came bursting into the private booth, dragging the blonde away despite her protests.

"Let's go!" the redhead yelled, earning a scowl from the blonde.

"What?"

"We need to go. Come on!"

They were gone before he could react, but part of him felt an incredible sense of relief that circumstances had stopped him before things had gone too far. As much as he'd wanted her, he'd known it wasn't a good idea to sleep with her.

"Where did she go?" Jack questioned, coming out of the booth next to Eli's.

"Gone," Eli responded with a shrug, patting his friend on the shoulder.

Jack looked simultaneously frustrated and amused. "Is everything okay?" Eli asked. Jack gave him a pained look in response.

"She puked on me!" he cried in disgust as he checked his pants. Eli burst into laughter. No wonder the redhead had been in such a rush. She must have been embarrassed.

"Come on," he said, leading Jack back to the bar. "Plenty of fish in the sea, right? The night's still young."

But Eli knew he was lying to himself about wanting to meet anyone else. Not after he'd had a taste of the mystery blonde.

4

It had been three days since Meredith had arrived back in her hometown. As per her agreement with her father, she would be spending her entire summer working in D.C., although she still didn't know the details. He'd just smiled and urged her to be patient when she'd asked him about it. She hoped everything would turn out fine regarding their deal.

Ideally the next few months would fly by, and then she'd be partying hard overseas.

Sitting at the large dining table, Meredith ate her breakfast, enjoying the solitude before her parents inevitably came to join her. She was starting to miss Lily. And she couldn't help but think of how nice the weather in Bali must be right about now.

Relax. You made the right choice, she reminded herself.

It wasn't long before Meredith's mother showed up. Elizabeth Howard Fields favored her daughter She had long, wavy blonde hair which was usually styled into an elegant bun. Like Meredith, her eyes were an unusual ocean blue color. Elizabeth was slim and if not for her mature personality, nobody would even think she had two children, with Meredith being the eldest at twenty-three.

"Good morning, honey," Elizabeth greeted Meredith warmly as she took a seat across the table. She was smiling at her as if they hadn't seen each other for a very long time.

Well they hadn't, or at least not until three days ago, technically speaking.

"Morning, Mom," Meredith responded before taking a bite of the toast she was holding.

"How's settling in going?" her mom asked, nodding pleasantly at the maid who was pouring her a glass of ice water.

"Fine," she replied, then shrugged. "I guess," Meredith added, quite unsure.

She didn't have the faintest clue about what her dad had in store for her. All she knew was that she wanted the summer to pass as quickly as possible, and that she couldn't wait for her trust fund to finally be released. By then, she would be free to do whatever she wanted.

But you want to be a journalist. This is what you've always wanted, whispered her inner voice, which made her mentally groan.

It was true that she wanted to be a successful reporter. It had been a goal of hers since she was little. But she'd just graduated from college! She deserved a break, didn't she?

"You guess? Did you leave something important back in New York?" her mom asked teasingly, eyeing Meredith with a playful grin on her lips. "Or maybe someone?"

Meredith chuckled and shook her head. Her mom was being a little silly, but she had to admit that some part of her thought having someone waiting for her back in the city would be nice.

Unbidden, the image of a masked man came to mind. Specifically, the man she'd met at the party with Lily. He'd had the most beautiful grey eyes she'd ever seen. And she was certain that he would have met all her expectations if he'd removed his mask that night.

God, how she wished she had seen his face.

She knew she'd been drunk that night, but for some reason he remained vivid in her mind, along with the effect he'd had on her body. If Lily hadn't come to whisk her away, she probably would have slept with that total stranger.

It was crazy.

It gave her goosebumps just thinking about it. She'd always been so careful when it came to dealing with members of the opposite sex. But that night, she'd been willing to give it up to someone whose face she hadn't even seen – with a complete stranger!

It was as if a spell had been cast on her as she'd stared deep into his grey orbs.

It had all felt so very... magical.

Ew. Magical, my ass. You were drunk and desperate. You would have given it up to anyone for all you know, a mocking voice in her head said. Realistically, she knew this assessment probably wasn't too far off the mark.

"Honey? Is something bothering you?" Elizabeth asked, giving Meredith a questioning look. She appeared curious and worried at the same time.

"Huh?" Meredith blinked after being pulled back to reality. She averted her gaze and stared fixedly at her plate.

"So, you do have someone!" Her mother shot her a triumphant, knowing look.

"What? Mom!" she groaned, then heaved a deep sigh. "There's no one, okay? I wish though."

"Fine," Elizabeth said, but her tone suggested she didn't quite believe Meredith. She smiled, clearly having fun.

"Let's just eat," Meredith mumbled and smiled, still embarrassed by the sudden question.

"Oh, come on, honey. You know you can tell me anything. How's your stay been so far?"

Meredith rolled her eyes. "It would have been better if I'd gone to Bali with Lily."

"It's not too late to change your mind, dear," Elizabeth spoke mischievously, giving her a wink. Her mom had always pushed for her daughters to enjoy their youth. It was probably because she'd married at such a young age.

"Seriously? Are you sure you're my mother? You sound just like Lily," Meredith said, shaking her head when Elizabeth just giggled. Sometimes she couldn't believe the things her mother would say in private, when in public she was very much prim and proper. They lapsed into a comfortable silence as they worked on finishing their respective breakfasts.

"Are you going to work today?" her mom asked abruptly, sending shivers down her spine.

Today would be her first day working at her dad's company – the New York Tribune. And as much as she hated the idea of spending her entire summer back home, she couldn't help but feel a little excited.

From this point on, she would no longer be an intern, nor a student. Today she would be able to put all of her knowledge to use and hopefully gain more experience.

"Yep," she responded, careful to keep her tone neutral. She didn't want her mom to think she wasn't taking things seriously.

"Are you sure you can handle it? It's not going to be easy, Meredith," her mother said gently.

"Mom, I chose this. Whether it's easy or not, I'm going to do this. This is what I've always wanted to do, remember?"

Elizabeth nodded, but kept silent. She'd always been more easygoing than her father.

They resumed eating as another comfortable silence settled between them. After several moments had passed, her father appeared, dressed formally in a suit and tie as usual.

"Good morning," her father greeted with a smile.

Where Meredith's mother was petite and blonde, her father was tall and dark. Meredith might not have inherited any of his physical characteristics, but she took after him in personality.

"Good morning," Mer and Elizabeth chorused in turn.

Sipping from his favorite coffee mug, her dad eyed Meredith, who was finally finished eating.

"Are you ready?" Benedict asked suddenly, startling her as she neatly dabbed at the corners of her mouth with her napkin.

She didn't feel ready. But she couldn't admit that to her dad, especially not after the deal they'd struck.

"Yes," she heard herself say, rising from her seat with a smile and turning to retrieve the garment bag that was neatly draped on the chair next to her. She'd asked their maid to press her favorite Chanel pantsuit to wear for her first day of work. But the smile on her lips vanished when her father let out a hearty laugh.

"What?" she asked, puzzled.

"You're going to need more than that, honey." Meredith exchanged a confused glance with her mother.

"She graduated from Columbia," Elizabeth said pointedly.

"She did. But it's better not to show off, don't you think?" Benedict responded calmly. Elizabeth frowned.

"So wearing what she wants is showing off somehow?" her mother said, folding her arms across her chest.

Her mother loved fashion and owned several boutiques stocked with garments from only the most exclusive, in-demand designers. Meredith had a keen interest in fashion as well, thanks to her mother's influence. But her mother seemed to be taking this almost personally.

Her dad closed his eyes and pinched the bridge of his nose. Meredith and her mother exchanged glances again while they waited for him to respond.

"It's too flashy," he finally said, opening his eyes and shaking his head.

Meredith didn't want her parents to fight. Yes, her mother was mostly easygoing, but when it came to certain topics she knew her mother would never back down. She cleared her throat, and both her parents turned to look at her.

"What should I wear then?" she asked, feeling slightly disappointed that she wouldn't be able to wear her favorite clothes to work. But she did want to fit in.

Silence filled the room as he looked her over thoughtfully. Meredith lowered her head when she felt her cheeks growing hot from his intense scrutiny, realizing she was wearing gym clothes despite having skipped her morning workout earlier in favor of getting more sleep.

"That will do," her dad commented, referring to her outfit.

"Seriously?" she asked, quite taken aback. If the pantsuit was too flashy, surely this outfit was too casual by comparison?

"Yes. Keep in mind you'll be on your feet a lot throughout the day, and you'll want to be comfortable. You'll thank me later," he said with a wink. Meredith rolled her eyes. That was one of his favorite phrases to use on her and her sister. But she couldn't think of a single time where he'd said that, and not been right.

Nodding in response, Meredith headed to her room to finish getting ready. By the time she headed downstairs again, her parents were already waiting for her in the foyer.

"Shall we?" she said with a wide smile on her face. She couldn't suppress the feeling of excitement as her dad led the way to the garage, where their private driver waited.

"Have a lovely day dear," her mom whispered, giving her a light kiss on the cheek.

"Elizabeth, she'll be fine. I'm with her," Benedict murmured softly, shaking his head before kissing her mom on the temple.

"She should be. I'm counting on you."

"I'm going to be just fine, you guys. I'm not a kid anymore," Meredith piped up, shaking her head. Her parents chuckled, and exchanged their goodbyes.

Soon Meredith and her father were on their way. Meredith looked out the window, noting all the myriad changes to the neighborhood where she'd spent her entire life until leaving for college. Some buildings she'd expected to see had been replaced by newer, taller structures. The park where she'd played with friends in elementary school was gone, replaced by a cafe.

She smiled. Things had changed. But so had she.

She had grown up.

With a start, she realized she didn't recognize the path the driver was taking. She frowned and turned to her father.

"Where are we going?" she asked, wondering what he had planned. Maybe she wouldn't be working in the main office after all.

Her dad smiled and winked at her.

"Where were you planning on going if you hadn't come home for the summer? And where are you planning on going once the summer is over?"

Meredith froze. She hadn't expected to discuss this so soon. And definitely not with her dad.

"I was going to go to Bali with Lily. She's there right now," she said. "And I guess I'll head to Europe and meet her wherever she ends up when summer's over," she added.

"I see," he said, looking thoughtful. Meredith wondered what he was thinking.

"Okay. You can go. On one condition…"

"What condition?" she asked cautiously. She didn't want to get her hopes up prematurely if he was going to ask her for something impossible.

"I want you to report on the presidential campaign. Use your degree for the whole summer and you're free to go," he said.

"Really? That's it?"

His lips quirked up into a smile.

"That's it," he said. "Oh, and make sure you call your parents from time to time," he added.

"I will! And thank you Dad!" she exclaimed happily, giving him a hug.

"You're welcome. But it's not all going to be fun and games, Meredith. Working a presidential campaign isn't an easy assignment. And you'll be representing the company, so you'll need to be on your best behavior at all times."

She nodded. "Dad, I know. Trust me." Besides, she thought, it doesn't matter as long as I get to Bali after this is all done.

Shaking his head, her dad handed her a file with all the information she would need about this assignment. She was too excited to even spare it a single glance before shoving the papers inside her bag.

Bali! Wait for me! she thought enthusiastically.

Shortly, the car stopped in front of an unfamiliar office building. Meredith got out of the car and hurried alongside her father, following his lead.

A stunning brunette was waiting for them. Meredith learned that her name was Sosie, and she was the manager for the campaign. She ushered them toward the candidate's office, making pleasant small talk with her father. Meredith relaxed and spaced out a bit, daydreaming about Bali. She could practically feel the hot sand under her toes already.

She shook her head. She needed to start taking this seriously. She peeked into her bag and hurriedly scanned the file her father had given her. It wouldn't do to be completely ignorant. But all she had time to see was the candidate's name – Elijah Scott. It wasn't familiar to her though. *Probably some old married guy*, she thought.

As they stepped into a spacious office, she idly hoped she wouldn't die from sheer boredom over the next few months.

"Mr. Fields of the New York Tribune is here," Sosie informed the man who was sitting on an office chair, looking out the windows.

Meredith felt fluttering in her stomach as the tall figure rose from his seat. Taller than even her father by a few inches, his shoulders were broad, and she could tell his muscular physique was the product of frequent trips to the gym.

As he turned to greet them, she found herself holding her breath. He looked way too young to be a presidential candidate. And in fact, she thought he looked more like a model than a career politician.

Tall, dark, and handsome, just her type. She was captivated by his presence. She'd never expected to be working with someone so young, let alone so handsome. He was sinfully handsome.

Is he married? she wondered to herself.

"Good morning, Mr. Fields. It's so good to see you again," Elijah said warmly, shaking her father's hand.

"The pleasure is all mine, Mr. Scott," her father responded in a friendly tone.

"Please, Elijah is just fine. Mr. Scott is my father."

Meredith heard her father chuckle. "Elijah it is. This is my daughter Meredith. She'll be working on the campaign trail with you like we discussed," he said, taking a seat and motioning for her to join him on the couch.

Meredith obediently took a seat next to her father, feeling slightly awkward when Elijah looked at her. When their eyes met, she felt butterflies flutter in her stomach. Something about his gaze was making her feel nervous for some reason.

But at the same time, something about him seemed strangely familiar...

It was his eyes. She could look at them all day. They were an unusual shade of grey. She knew they had never met before, so why did she have this nagging feeling like she somehow knew him already?

"It's nice to meet you, Meredith," Elijah greeted her warmly, offering his hand for her to shake. He smiled.

When she shook his hand, she felt positively electric. The truth finally hit her when the image of the masked man from the party popped into her head.

The man from the party was the same person standing in front of her.

It's him!

5

*M*eredith.

Elijah was completely stunned when he realized he was staring at the woman who had been haunting his dreams for days now. The woman he'd been fantasizing about nonstop since the party.

After the party, not a single day had passed where he hadn't spent every moment of his limited free time picturing her lying underneath him, calling his name, writhing and moaning. Or her on her knees, wrapping those perfectly pouty lips around his cock.

He almost couldn't believe who she was. Eldest daughter of the Benedict Percival Fields of the New York Tribune. Now he was finally and completely convinced it was a good thing nothing had happened between them at the party. His political career could be over in a flash if he got involved with her.

Small world, huh? his inner voice whispered sarcastically as he averted his gaze, careful to pretend like he was only just now meeting Meredith for the first time.

"I'm so pleased you'll be the one showing my Meredith around. I trust you'll make sure she'll be in good hands," Benedict Fields stated.

Eli couldn't help feeling a little ashamed. He hoped his face hadn't given away all the perverted thoughts he'd been having about Meredith just now.

"It's my pleasure to have her with us, Mr. Fields," he said, trying to shove the thoughts out of his mind. He nodded and smiled, trying to reassure him his daughter would be in good hands.

After a few more minutes, Benedict Fields said goodbye, leaving Meredith behind for orientation with Sosie. Eli wasn't sure what to do when Sosie received an important phone call she'd been expecting, stepping out of the office and leaving him alone with Meredith.

Still trying to play it cool, he sat back on his chair and directed his attention out the window. He was trying to come to terms with the fact that Meredith would be a part of his campaign. But he was dreading the inevitable conversation they were going to have; he could tell Meredith had recognized him from the party, mask or not.

So much for that supposed anonymity, he thought.

If she asks, just play dumb and act like you don't know anything. Simple, his inner voice said.

Something told him it wouldn't be that simple though as he turned and saw Meredith staring at him. Thankfully Sosie stepped back into the office a few seconds later, ready to take Meredith around the offices for her orientation.

Eli's relief was short-lived, however. Before he knew it, Sosie was back on the phone, and Meredith was in his office once more. She shot him a questioning look, folding her arms across her chest. He decided to try and take control of the situation. "Is there something I can help you with, Miss Fields?" he asked coolly.

"It was you," she said in a hushed whisper, eyebrow raised. She sounded completely certain.

Yep, it was me. What's it to you? said the devil in his mind.

Aloud he asked, "What do you mean?" hoping his face didn't betray his nerves. Usually around journalists he was able to lie with impunity like any good politician, but this woman was different.

Meredith narrowed her eyes and shot him a suspicious glare.

"You were the man I met at the masquerade party in New York, weren't you?" she pressed on, demanding an answer. This time she planted her hands on her hips, making him groan mentally.

Seeing Meredith in tight leggings that hugged her curves in all the right places, Eli couldn't help but check out her body. And fuck, just from looking at her he was already growing hard.

"I don't know what you're talking about, Miss Fields," he said, trying to disarm her with a boyish smile. He was doing his best to keep his face straight until her curiosity subsided.

She opened her mouth to reply, but just then Sosie came back into the room, whisking Meredith away again. Eli couldn't help staring at her ass as she walked away. He shook his head. What was he thinking? She needed to go.

If the public were to find out he'd attended what was essentially an anonymous sex party, that would be the end of his career. It wasn't like he could tell Benedict Fields or Sosie the truth either. He'd just have to come up with an excuse to have Meredith removed from the campaign.

He didn't want to kick her off the campaign, but that was the best plan he could come up with in order to save face and keep his career intact from possible scandal.

Eli's thoughts were a jumbled mess when he heard a knock at the door. It was Henry, carrying a couple of boxes containing flyers.

"What's up?" he asked, putting the boxes on the floor.

Taking a deep sigh, Eli slumped against the couch, earning a frown from his friend.

"Meredith Fields, daughter of Benedict Fields of the New York Tribune, will be working on the campaign," he murmured helplessly.

Henry crumpled up his face in confusion. "So? Why the long face?"

Shooting up from his seat, Eli strode across the room and shut the door to his office. He didn't want to take any chances that anyone would overhear what he was about to say.

"She was the girl who was with me in the private booth that night at the party. She gave me a fucking lap dance," he explained in exasperation, looking more frustrated than ever.

Henry fell silent, baffled.

"The blonde? Her? Here?"

"Yeah. Un-fucking-believable, right?" he said, shaking his head.

"What are you going to do?" Henry asked.

"I knew I shouldn't have gone to that party. I just..." Eli trailed off as images of a drunk yet incredibly sexy Meredith Fields flooded his mind. "I have to find a way to get her reassigned or something. I can't trust a journalist to stay quiet about a scoop like this, right?"

Instead of agreeing, Henry just gave him a thoughtful look..

"What?" Eli asked, annoyed.

"Nothing. It's just… you know, if you like her…"

Eli scoffed. He couldn't believe Henry would even say that. Besides, he knew next to nothing about her. He'd have to get to know her to know if he liked her or not. But at the same time, he couldn't deny he was physically attracted to Meredith Fields. Very much so.

"It's not a matter of liking her or not. I can't afford to get involved with a journalist. You know the other parties are already running oppo on me," he explained patiently, reminding himself that unlike him, Henry was not a career politician. "I can't give them any reasons to pry into my private life further."

"Okay, okay, I get it, geez," Henry said, shaking his head. "Anyway, I'll see you later. I've got an appointment."

"What appointment?" Eli asked curiously.

"Psych."

"A psych appointment?" he repeated, earning a scowl from Henry.

"Hey. Stop being so loud. That's just between us, you know."

"Alright, go on. But there's nothing to be embarrassed of," Eli stated.

Henry just grunted and left, leaving the office door open behind him. Elijah hovered in the doorway, watching Sosie and Meredith interacting with other staffers.

When Sosie turned to look at him, Eli found himself averting his gaze. She approached him with a curious look on her face.

"What's on your mind?" Sosie asked.

"Miss Fields is very young. She's too inexperienced," he replied, fighting the urge to take back what he'd just said.

Sosie snorted.

"Her father is Benedict Fields. She may be young, yes, but I don't think she's inexperienced. It would be stupid to replace her," she stated confidently.

And as much as he wanted to argue with her, he couldn't. She was right, of course.

"But we need to," he said, not sure how to explain things to Sosie and hoping she wouldn't pry the truth out of him.

"Why?" she said, giving him a suspicious glare.

"She knows something about me that could mean the end of my campaign," he mumbled, hoping that was enough for Sosie to go on. "And I'm not sure she'll stay quiet about it."

Sosie looked confused, but remained silent. When she'd recovered her composure, she went through a list of things she thought might mean the end of the campaign. Thankfully none of them were close to the truth, but he didn't appreciate her digging either.

"No! Stop guessing," he said, feeling irritable.

Having Meredith Fields around would mean battling constant temptation. He was starting to wonder if he would be able to focus on the campaign, knowing she would be in the same building with him.

Fuck.

"Is this something I need to know about?" Sosie asked abruptly, narrowing her eyes at him. "I can't protect your campaign if you don't tell me the truth, Eli."

He sighed and shook his head.

"No. But get rid of her," he said.

It was Sosie's turn to sigh heavily and shake her head.

"I can't, Elijah. I can't tell the biggest publishing magnate in the country that his daughter isn't good enough. No matter what excuse I use, you know as well as I do that's how he's going to take it. Benedict Fields is a very powerful man. Whatever your secret is, do you think it's worth having the New York Tribune go after you?"

Eli fell silent.

She was right.

Pissing off Meredith's father would also mean the death of his political career, just in a different way. By all accounts Benedict Fields was an intensely private man, but two things were certain. He loved his wife and daughters above all else in the world, and he was certainly no pushover.

Eli's hands balled into fists. He felt like he'd been back into a corner with no way out. There was absolutely nothing he could do about Meredith. He'd have to settle for denying everything about that night.

If only he could deny his attraction to her as well.

"No," he responded to Sosie grudgingly.

Turning on her heels, his campaign manager gave him a pointed look before walking back to the other trainees. Eli gave Sosie a curt nod before scowling at Meredith, who was still staring at him and frowning. Cursing under his breath, he retreated within his office and shut the door.

6

Meredith rubbed at her eyes and let out a huge yawn. It had still been dark out and everyone else had still been sleeping except for the maid and her driver. She'd been up much later than usual, trying to convince her dad that she didn't want this particular assignment anymore.

Initially he'd thought she was kidding. He laughed, telling her he appreciated her attempts at what surely had to be a joke. But when he realized she wasn't joking, he'd brooked no further conversation about the matter. "A Fields never backs down from a challenge," he'd said to her, as he had many times throughout her entire life.

Scowling at the memory, she took a quick mental inventory of what she'd packed. Space on the campaign bus would be limited, and Sosie had instructed her to pack light, limiting her to one suitcase. She'd opted to bring mostly interchangeable separates she could create multiple outfits from, with not a single pantsuit in the bunch.

She looked out the window and watched the sunrise, feeling gloomier than ever. She didn't know why, but she had a bad feeling about this campaign.

It was definitely him. I can't be wrong, she thought as images of the masked man and Elijah Scott overlapped in her mind.

After being introduced to Elijah, she'd wanted to run out of his office and never look back. Elijah Scott was without a doubt the man she'd given a lap dance to her last night in New York. Even worse, she knew he'd recognize her, since she'd removed her mask. She was sure her father would have a heart attack if he knew about any of that.

Embarrassment had been eating away at her since then.

But for all his insistence, she knew he was just pretending not to know her. Not that she could blame him – after all, he was just doing his best to protect his image. Maybe she could catch him in private and clear the air between them. She was sure she could get him to agree to just forget about it, for both their sakes.

Slowly exhaling, Meredith couldn't deny the fact she was strongly attracted to the handsome bachelor. Just like she couldn't deny she'd wished her father had agreed to pull her off this assignment.

She couldn't believe how complicated her life had become over the past few days. This wasn't part of her summer plans. And it definitely wasn't what she wanted.

When she arrived, Meredith hurried to take her place with the other journalists who were already present, furtively looking around for Elijah Scott's familiar figure.

After looking around twice, she still didn't see him. Maybe he was already on the bus? She wanted to scold herself when she realized she was actually disappointed at not seeing him. She had a job to do, one that didn't involve lusting after Elijah Scott, no matter how hot he was.

She was representing her father's company. He'd made that crystal clear last night.

Get your act together, Meredith! she quietly admonished herself as she stepped onto the bus.

She took a seat near the center of the bus, hoping placing herself in the middle of the action would help distract her from obsessing over Elijah. Everyone already seemed to be working, their heads bent over laptops and notepads, and she followed suit, trying to fit in.

A few moments later Sosie stepped onto the bus, followed by a middle-aged man she introduced as Edward, their driver. Sosie had everyone's full attention as she went over the rules. Meredith listened attentively, not wanting to get on Sosie's bad side.

Sosie reminded everyone the only stops the bus would make would be those planned out ahead of time, listed on the itinerary she'd already emailed to everyone. Loud talking and listening to music without headphones would be prohibited, due to the fact they would be busy working while they were traveling.

"I think that's all I have to say for now," Sosie said in conclusion. "But I do have a surprise for all of you," she added, gesturing to the door of the bus.

Elijah Scott entered the bus, and Meredith held her breath as their eyes met. He was wearing a white polo and dark grey slacks, and looked as handsome as ever.

"Eli's going to ride on this bus with you guys for the first leg of the trip. Now's your chance to make a good impression," she said, looking at all of them in turn, eyes lingering on Meredith for maybe just a split second longer. Or maybe Meredith had just imagined that.

Meredith couldn't stop staring at him despite herself. He was just too hot for his own good.

Damn. Why does he have to be so gorgeous?

A disturbing thought suddenly occurred to her. She belatedly realized Sosie had made eye contact with her much more than any of the other campaign staffers or journalists as she'd been giving out instructions. It had been weird.

Oh my God! Did he tell Sosie about me and that night?

"That's it. Good luck, everyone. See you at the hotel," Sosie said, then got off the bus.

Meredith wasn't sure what to do. She could practically feel Elijah staring at her from across the bus as he took a seat near the front. Her cheeks grew hot when she realized she wanted him to stare at her, wanted his attention.

As the bus departed, Elijah smiled and began answering questions from the other journalists present. Meredith opened her laptop and started taking notes, hoping to distract herself with work. But her mind kept wandering.

It was stupid.

Biting her bottom lip, she remembered how good it had felt to have his strong arms wrapped around her. She remembered how hard his cock had been as she'd danced on his lap.

She wondered how long and thick he was. Thanks to him, she couldn't stop having thoughts like this..

Snickering from the back of the bus brought her back to reality. "Miss Fields?" she heard Eli say. Judging by the response, he'd been trying to get her attention for some time now.

"Sorry, what?" she asked, perplexed.

Elijah tilted his head, and she felt her stomach twisting into knots as everyone turned to look at her.

"I said, do you have a question for me, Miss Fields? Other than the one you just asked, of course," he said with a grin, eliciting loud laughter from the other journalists.

Flustered, she racked her brain to come up with something.

"What kind of outfits do you prefer for summer? More casual, or more formal?" she blurted without thinking.

Meredith froze when she realized what she'd just asked. She'd had a chance to ask him anything, and that question had been pure fluff. So much for being a real journalist.

She felt even more pathetic when Elijah actually humored her with a legitimate answer.

"I don't have specific clothing preferences. I wear whatever a particular situation calls for," he said, already moving on to take the next question.

Feeling thoroughly and utterly humiliated, she directed her attention back to her laptop, pretending to take notes when in reality she was berating herself.

Gritting her teeth, she cursed Elijah under her breath.

7

$\mathcal{E}$lijah drummed his fingers against his thigh as he looked out the window of the limo. There was still so much that needed to be done today, but he was feeling exceptionally lazy, which was rare for him.

He had to make some revisions on the speech he'd be giving at the next campaign rally, and he needed to have his suits dry cleaned. Maybe if he hit the gym he wouldn't feel quite so lethargic. Working out sounded way more appealing than being cooped up working in his hotel suite.

When the limo came to a stop in front of the hotel where he and his campaign team were staying, he got down immediately.

"I'd like to be alone," he instructed his security team, who immediately complied. Of course they weren't actually leaving him by himself, but they could give him the illusion of privacy.

Upon reaching his suite, Elijah

changed into his gym clothes. Maybe working out would take his mind off of Meredith, at least for a little while. He hoped, anyway. He wanted to groan at what he saw when he entered the gym.

Meredith was on an elliptical, chatting away with another journalist named Ava next to her. They were pleasantly chatting away. It sounded like Meredith was telling a story about someone named Lily.

Eli found himself amused as he listened to her story, but she stopped talking abruptly when she saw him.

He smiled, feeling slightly embarrassed after being caught eavesdropping.

"Don't mind me," he said with a smile, pointing at a treadmill before putting in his headphones. He hoped they'd continue on like he wasn't even there.

But they went silent.

Ava was first to leave, shooting him a look on her way out.

Was that supposed to be seductive? he thought.

Without saying anything, Meredith moved to a treadmill and began jogging. She looked like she was taking her workout seriously, but he couldn't stop admiring her body in her gym clothes.

Feeling like now was as good a time as any to broach the subject about that night at the party since they were the only two people in the gym, Eli slowed his pace. He had to make sure she wouldn't write a tell-all on him.

"So, have you forgotten about the masquerade?" he asked, breaking the silence.

Meredith paused in surprise, completely forgetting she was on a treadmill. She tripped and went down hard, yelling out in shock and pain.

Instantly, he stopped his treadmill to check on her. He carefully scooped her up and laid her on a flat weight bench.

Eli started to feel his pulse racing when their eyes locked. The more he looked at her, the more he found her beautiful.

Nobody had ever made him feel like this before.

Yes, she was hot as fuck, but there was something special about her, something more to this than just his lust...

Something he couldn't explain every time their eyes met.

I must be out of my mind, he thought, looking away when she slipped from his grasp.

"What?" she asked awkwardly. "Do I have something on my face?"

He knew she wasn't immune to his presence either. It was crystal clear she was attracted to him just as much as he was to her.

"I was wondering why you haven't mentioned that night again," he answered, moving on as if nothing had happened. He was starting to think his acting skills had gotten better.

"I— I— I haven't forgotten," she answered stammering, looking away to conceal the redness of her cheeks.

Eli couldn't suppress the smile that formed on his lips as he watched her. One moment she was a seductress, and the next thing he knew, she was a cute teenager. How could she possibly flit between the two without making him think she was pretending?

"No? Are you sure?"

"I just… you know, the story doesn't paint me in a flattering light either," she murmured shyly, turning to check out her left ankle.

He felt his cock twitch when he saw her twist at the waist, exposing her cleavage. It wasn't like it was his first time seeing a sexy woman or her breasts. But he felt like a horny teenager all over again, always turned on and unable to control it.

Damn her for being so fucking hot.

And damn him for lusting over someone he couldn't have.

"I guess? But only if you were honest about it. I don't know you, Meredith. How do I know you won't tell the story in a way where you come off completely innocent, and I look like some pervert?" he asked. He hated phrasing things this way, but he needed to see what kind of journalist she was.

He knew how the world worked. If Meredith wanted to get noticed, a scandal about him would be a good start.

She frowned, eyeing him like he'd just said something completely ludicrous.

"I wouldn't do that," she stated firmly.

"Again, I don't know about that. You have to admit that you showing up to work on my campaign…" he paused, stealing another glance at her beautiful face. "Well, a skeptical man could draw some unfavorable conclusions."

She chuckled dryly before straightening her body. Crossing her arms over her chest, she looked him straight in the eyes without any trace of anxiety or awkwardness. Her jaw tensed, and he could tell he had touched a nerve. But he liked this side of her.

"Are you a skeptical man?" she questioned, arching an eyebrow.

Eli fell silent for a moment, then smiled.

"I prefer to be cautious," he replied.

"Except for sex parties, of course," she added, making him grin.

"Except then it seems," he agreed.

He wanted to smack himself when he'd realized what he'd just said. She'd managed to convince him to discuss something he should be refusing to talk about, especially with her. He should have known he'd be defenseless against her charms – just like that night.

"Why even go then?" she pressed. He looked at her, and she was holding a towel, wiping away her sweat.

Eli had to bite his tongue to suppress the groan that threatened to leave his lips when she tilted her head to dry her neck. It was like he was watching her move in slow motion. He had the sudden urge to lean over and lick the beads of sweat off of her exposed cleavage.

Fuck.

"I guess I thought I'd have one last hurrah before hitting the campaign trail," he admitted.

He turned and went back onto the treadmill. What was he thinking? If she planned on ruining his career, she had more than enough ammunition to use against him.

"One last chance to be bad?" she guessed.

"One last chance to be myself," he corrected her. "Unbound," he added with a smirk. He was trying his best not to spare her even a single glance while she continued to pat herself dry with that towel. If he did, he knew for certain he'd be the one falling off the treadmill this time.

"I see," she said. She paused, then continued, saying, "I think you should know I had no idea who you even were until the day before yesterday. I know you don't know me very well, but..." She trailed off, then shook her head. "I suppose you'll just have to take my word for it."

With that, Eli decided working out was a bust for today. There was no point in him trying to stop thinking about Meredith when she was standing just a few feet away from him.

Looking her straight in the eyes, he took a few large strides toward her, closing the distance between them quickly.

"Is that right?" he asked.

Lost and confused, Eli found his fingertips hovering a hair's breadth from touching Meredith's mouth, which was slightly parted. Her pink lips looked luscious as usual. And he wanted desperately to kiss her.

God, how he'd love to kiss her.

He grit his teeth when he saw her throat's fluttering pulse. But he knew too well that she was just waiting for him to make a move.

Oh, man. I'm doomed, he thought when she swallowed hard.

"That's right," she spoke in almost a whisper, snapping him back to reality.

"I... I should go. We have an early morning tomorrow," she said, grabbing her water bottle and leaving without another word.

Cursing himself yet again, he watched her go, unabashedly checking her out.

It wasn't a crime to look, right?

8

od, you're so hot," he mumbled against her skin, nibbling her side.

Meredith smiled and caressed his cheek. The room was cold, but her touch burned like fire. She was looking at him with pure desire as his hands cupped her breasts.

"Fuck me," she whispered pleadingly.

He looked deep into her eyes as he wrapped his arms around her tiny waist, feeling her body heat as her breasts rubbed against his hard chest. God, he had been waiting so long for this moment to happen. And he was pleased beyond belief to finally have her beneath him.

Leaning in, he kissed her slowly and tenderly, savoring her desire and feeding her lust. Her lips were soft and delicious. But he didn't mind taking his time. She was finally in his arms, and no one could stop him from making love to her.

"Mmmm…" Meredith moaned, arching her back.

His hands traveled down her body, squeezing her ass hard, earning himself a little bite on the lower lip. And he liked it. She was so fucking playful, his little tease.He ached to get inside her. He couldn't believe that this was finally happening. And he didn't care about anything other than enjoying it fully and making this moment memorable.

He was naked and kissing Meredith. It was all that mattered.

Pulling her closer, he kissed her desperately. And he was more than delighted when she responded with the same intensity. He wanted to make her feel special – to feel loved.

And he wanted her more than anything and anyone in the world.

When he was about to push her back onto the soft mattress, she moved quickly, switching their positions with him so that he was underneath her. He was shocked at how she was capable of doing that with such a small figure.

"Relax," she whispered seductively before pulling away from his grasp.

Watching her walk toward the dresser, he swallowed hard as his eyes roamed her body. He had imagined her nude countless times, but seeing her like this was infinitely more exciting.

He licked his lips when she dragged a chair to the foot of the bed. And excitement rocked his entire being when she gestured for him to sit on it. They were both naked, and his cock was rock hard.

Like a replay of how they first met, she sat on his lap and began grinding against him. Her wet pussy rubbed against his thighs, and her breasts bounced in front of him, though she wouldn't allow him to touch her, not yet. He grunted when she touched his cock, stroking it up and down.

"You like that, huh?" she whispered naughtily when a loud groan of pleasure escaped his lips.

Damn. She felt so fucking great.

"Fuck! Yes!" he answered, eager for more.Driven to the edge of bliss, she pulled his head down to her breasts as her hips moved back and forth. This time, her wet pussy teased the tip of his cock. Feeling half insane from desire, he sucked on her breasts.

"Ahhh… Ohh… Mmmm…" she moaned in pleasure, enjoying the sensations his mouth had brought. She leaned closer and her hips moved faster to gain more friction, and he could tell that she, too, was growing impatient.

Pulling away, he seared her mouth with a kiss and squeezed her ass. He lifted her weight a little, just enough so her wet pussy hovered over his cock. He thought he could to do it her way, but he was fucking horny and he badly needed to feel her around him.

He slid a finger in between her thighs and touched her clit, giving her a little taste of heaven. Then he stopped.

"You like that, huh?" he teased, imitating her. He pulled his finger out of her and brought it to his mouth. She tasted so good, so sweet. And he wanted more.

With narrowed eyes, Meredith placed both of her hands on his shoulder. And in one swoop, she sat on his lap, her pussy fully sucking on his hard cock. He was surprised with the sudden aggression. But pleased when she started moving her hips, trying to accommodate his length and thickness.

"Jesus!" he cried when she sped up.

"Oh, oh, oh…" she moaned. He could tell he was hitting her G-spot just right when her body arched as her walls quivered. She felt so fucking warm and tight around him.

He didn't think he'd ever get enough of her.

"Yes! Fuck me! Fuck me!" Meredith cried as he continued to thrust into her. He could feel himself getting close as his toes curled, and his muscles tensed.

But he didn't want to cum yet.

So he pulled out of her and scooped her tiny figure into his arms.

"Shit!" she cursed in annoyance, shooting him a deadly glare.

But he didn't mind.

He stopped in front of the dresser and slowly placed her atop it. Stepping between her legs, he pushed them wide open, completely exposing her. His hands caressed her legs, then he knelt down and feasted his eyes on her pussy. She was beautiful. He swallowed hard while looking at her dripping wet area. She was so fucking wet that he wanted to suck the juices out of her.

"What are you doing? Suck it," she ordered, pulling his head closer to her hole, making him grin at her impatience. "Do it hard, please," she added in a begging tone.

With that, he licked her with nothing but hunger. He could feel her fingers gripping his hair, and he knew she liked it.

Feeling proud, he slid his tongue inside her, sucking as hard as he could. He was no stranger to going down on a woman.

But with Meredith, it was new and exciting.

He watched her toes curling up as she gasped while moaning and screaming his name. When he sucked at her clit and kneaded her ass, she grunted and raked her fingernails across his back. He was finally acting out his sexual fantasies with Meredith, and the thought alone almost made him cum.

Pleased with her reactions, he slid two fingers inside of her as he continued licking her clit. And she wailed in ecstasy as he increased his pace, pushing in and out of her rapidly.

Hard and soft. Slow and fast. That was the rhythm he followed.

"Oooooohhhhh…" she moaned sexily as juices escaped her pussy, filling his mouth.

He licked every drop of her cum greedily. He'd do anything to make her happy.

She eyed him, biting her bottom lip mischievously. When she pulled him in for a kiss, he carried her back to the bed in his arms.

This time, it would be his turn.

He sat on the empty bed with Meredith still in his arms, her legs around his waist. He felt her bite his bottom lip, then she prompted him to lie flat on his back. Their tongues continued to probe and taste each other, and her hands traveled down to his throbbing cock.

He groaned when she showered him with tiny kisses, following the trail of tiny hairs from his chest down to his belly.

He gripped her hair when her mouth reached his balls. He could tell that she was grinning when she kissed the tip of his dick. He was acutely aware of his length and girth.

So, when he felt the warmth of her mouth around his penis, his eyes widened in a mixture of surprise and pleasure.

"Oh, fuck...!" he groaned, his grip tightening on her hair.

Yes, that made him feel so damn good.

She glanced at him as her mouth sucked his cock, swallowing his precum.

"Fuck!" he cursed again when she started rolling her tongue around him. And she drove him crazy when she slowly bobbed her head, sucking him hard with her cheeks hollowed.She sped up her movements, and his balls started to draw up to his body, as she sucked him down her throat faster each time.

He was getting close.He used all his remaining strength to get her beneath him, pulling his cock away from her heavenly mouth.

Impatiently, he spread her legs wide and thrust into her. He paused and waited for her to adjust to his fucking big cock, sheathing him with her juices. As she started moving underneath him, he held her arms above her head and took control.

He closed his eyes, enjoying how good it felt to have her tight pussy wrapped around him finally.

"Oh," she moaned, trying to match his pace. "Fuck me, Elijah," she begged as her hands pushed through his hair.

Her fingernails dug into his back once again and he begun to thrust in and out of her, pounding her with want and need.

She pulled his head closer to her body to make him suck on her tits. He happily obliged, sucking and biting the tips of her peaks as his mouth curled into a victorious smile.

"Make me cum, please!"

With that, he slammed in her as hard as he could, hitting her in all the right places, rotating his hips as she met his every thrust. And just when he was about to cum, he saw her eyelids flutter in bliss as sparks went off.

"Oh my god, Elijah!" she cried, her legs wrapping around him tighter, and her arms encircling his body.

He felt himself growing bigger inside her, and her walls quivered. They were nearing.

"Tell me to fuck you, Meredith," he ordered, thrusting into her harder than ever. He was almost out of breath, and was about to lose his mind as his muscles tensed.

"Fuck me hard!"

"Louder!"

"Fuck me hard, Elijah Scott!" she screamed, then lifted her body to meet him.

Meredith whimpered and shuddered in his arms as he continued to fuck her, drawing their orgasms out. When her body arched off the sheets, she cried out in pleasure before kissing him hard on the lips with his one last deep thrust to shoot his load.

They came together.

9

$\mathcal{E}$li shot up from bed, covered in a thin sheen of sweat.

"Shit!" he swore when he realized he was almost painfully hard. Of course he was. He'd just been dreaming about fucking Meredith in that very room.

Gritting his teeth, he got to his feet and headed for the bathroom. The more he tried to stop thinking about her, the harder and hotter he got. He needed a distraction.

He started the shower, shivering as he stepped under the icy cold spray. He hadn't needed to do this since he was a teenager.

Why are you doing this to me, Meredith?

His mind drifted as he showered, and he kept coming to the same conclusion, which was that it was impossible for them to be together. He couldn't risk everything he'd been working toward for years, not over a woman, even one like Meredith.

She was just too young for him.

He didn't want to imagine how the media would react to all of this.

It would be a mess if they ever found out the truth.

He closed his eyes, then groaned when he realized his erection hadn't subsided one bit. Wrapping his hand around his shaft, he began stroking his cock.

Images of Meredith popped into his head as he pumped his hand up and down the length. He knew it would feel a million times more amazing to be inside of her, but for now, this was all he could do.

God, how he wished his dream had been real. Remembering how they had cum together in the dream was enough to push him over the edge.

Eli groaned in relief as he found his release. Again, he'd probably been a teenager when he'd done this last, since he'd never had any problems getting laid, always having an endless slew of women to sleep with. He vowed he'd have his fill of sex once the election was over.

10

One whole week had passed since they'd left D.C. and hit the campaign trail. Meredith had been growing increasingly restless. She was still trying to cope with the sudden change in the lifestyle she'd known in college.

Sure, she was no stranger to sleep deprivation back in New York. But that had been due to late nights spent partying or studying. Here, her lack of sleep was all because of work. Being on the road constantly hadn't helped either.

Stepping off the bus, she dug in her bag for her phone and dialed Mitch, her editor. She needed to check in with him and report on all the information she'd gathered about Elijah Scott so far. It wasn't much, but maybe Mitch would find some of it useful.

Wheeling her suitcase into the hotel, Meredith's expression turned sour when she heard Mitch's only question for her.

"Have you heard anything about Elijah's love life?" he asked. She almost tripped and stumbled.

"Can't say that I have," Meredith replied, careful to keep her tone neutral. But her face must have given away her distress, since Sosie looked at her and frowned. Meredith quickly plastered a smile on her face and nodded as Sosie handed her the key to her room.

"Oh come on, Meredith. You have to have heard something by now. A guy like that is irresistible to women," he replied as she got in the elevator.

Of course he was irresistible to women. She had firsthand knowledge of that fact, not that she could tell Mitch how she'd come by that knowledge.

"I know, Mitch. But I haven't heard anything about it yet," she said apologetically. "Besides," she added, "I hardly even see Elijah." She hoped he would just drop it.

She got off the elevator on the fifteenth floor and quickly headed straight to her assigned room. She was so tired she just wanted to collapse into bed and sleep until tomorrow.

"Dig around some then, would you? See if you can get him alone. Do whatever it takes to make him talk. You know, use your charms," he suggested as she stopped in front of her room.

Meredith scowled, completely offended. What did he take her for?

She bit her tongue to keep from swearing at him. But she knew he hadn't meant anything by it. He was just doing his job, and part of that job was nagging the field reporters. God, she couldn't wait for this summer to just end already.

Meredith took a deep breath, trying to stay calm.

"I'll do it my way, Mitch. And you know as well as I do you wouldn't have suggested that if I were a guy," she grumbled.

He laughed, and she grit her teeth in annoyance.

"Don't take it personally, Mer. It's just part of the job. I know that every editor is asking their reporters the same thing."

"I know. And I understand. Look, I'll call you when I get something, okay?" she said, then hung up. She couldn't stand to hear any more nagging, especially when she already knew what needed to be done.

Getting inside her room, her mood lightened somewhat upon seeing the freshly made bed. Finally, she'd have some downtime alone. Forget about grabbing a shower and dinner – that was time she'd rather spend getting into pajamas and sleeping.

She checked the time, then flopped onto the bed. It was five in the afternoon. She thought she'd call Lily and see how she was doing. It had been awhile since they'd last talked.

After a few rings, Lily answered, sounding very hoarse and tired.

"Hello?"

"Hey. Is this a bad time?" Meredith asked when Lily's face registered on her screen. She looked disheveled, but still beautiful.

Lily yawned.

"No, no. I'm just about to go to bed, actually," she said, settling against a pillow.

"What? Didn't you just go to your yoga retreat?" Meredith asked. How late – or early – did her friend intend to stay awake?

"Hah! No. Bali is like… party central, Mer. Tonight, I went to this party on a billionaire's yacht… it was craaaaazy!" Lily informed her, her expression completely changing. She looked excited just by the thought of said gathering.

Meredith couldn't help but feel a twinge of jealousy. She should be there, living it up with Lily, not spending her summer working her ass off.

"Really?" she asked excitedly, wanting to hear about more of her friend's getaway trip.

"Yeah. Gosh, I'm going to need a yoga retreat after all this partying! It's exhausting," Lily replied after an exaggerated sigh, making her smile. "But enough about me, what about you? How's the life of a journalist?"

She rolled her eyes. She didn't want to talk about it. It wasn't like there was anything to brag about, unlike Lily's trip.

"Well, I'm on a presidential campaign…"

"And?"

"And… well, you absolutely can't say anything…"

"You already hooked up with someone, didn't you?" Lily interrupted.

"Let me finish, will you?" Meredith said, irritated.

"Okay," Lily responded, giggling.

"Hmm… remember your goodbye party?" she started out, not really sure how to properly spill the beans about Elijah Scott.

"Yeah."

"You can't tell anyone. Swear," Meredith said.

"I swear! Now tell me already!" the redhead ranted impatiently.

This wasn't going to be easy. But at least she had someone to talk to about it. She really needed someone to confide in, because the whole thing was driving her crazy.

Or more accurately, Elijah Scott was driving her crazy.

"I recognized someone here from the party," she said.

"What? Who?"

"The candidate. Elijah Scott," Meredith answered after a moment of silence. And she wanted to take back her words when Lily bolted up in bed. Her best friend was the one of the worst gossip girls she had ever known.

"Wait, really?"

"Yeah," she reaffirmed.

She'd thought about telling Lily that Elijah was the man she'd given a drunken lap dance to, the man she'd almost slept with that night. But Meredith decided not to say anything after all.

"No way. No freaking way! That's… what do the papers call it?" Lily said, completely losing it as she tried to search for the proper words. "A big scoop!" she said finally.

She rolled her eyes.

"Right, because I'm totally going to tell the world I was at a secret sex party," she said sarcastically. She added, "My dad would kill me, let's be real, Lily."

"Whatever," Lily said, pouting. Then she perked up. "Is he at least sexy?" she asked.

Meredith fell silent, picturing Elijah. His devastatingly handsome smile, his muscular physique.

Sexy didn't even begin to describe him.

"Holy shit! He totally is! I can tell by your expression!" Lily crowed.

There was no point in lying. Lily knew her all too well.

"Shut up."

"Ooohhhh, Mer and Elijah, sitting in a tree –"

"Okay. Okay. He's hot! But don't forget, you promised not to tell a soul. I mean it, Lily," she warned. Lily grinned.

"Cross my heart, hope to die," Lily replied, doing the corresponding hand gesture then yawned.

"Okay. I'm going to let you go. Call me sometime, though! I want to hear about all the fun I'm missing out while I'm on the trail," Meredith said, feeling guilty for postponing her best friend's beauty rest.

She was sure Lily's schedule was hectic. But unlike hers, each day would be filled with laughter and meeting new people. Endless drinking, dancing and partying. She was so freaking jealous of her!

Lily batted her lashes before pressing the bridge of her nose, fighting the urge to fall asleep immediately.

"Okay, I'll try not to get another best friend while you're off with Romeo," Lily teased, making her blush.

"Shut up."

"You shut up."

"Alright, bye," Meredith said with a smile before ending the call.

"Romeo, huh?" she said to herself, chuckling. *If only*, she thought.

Her thoughts were disturbed by a knock on her door. Quickly, she opened it and saw Sosie standing outside.

"Uh… hey," she greeted hesitantly, looking up and down the hall. Maybe Sosie had been looking for someone else and knocked on her door by mistake.

The woman eyed her for a moment, then handed her a garment bag. Meredith stared at it, confused.

"Get dressed. You're coming with us to a charity dinner tonight. You'll be taking Marie's spot; she isn't feeling well." Meredith didn't even think of trying to argue with Sosie. Not that Sosie would take no for an answer, she suspected.

"How long do I have to get ready?" she asked, awkwardly trying to hold the bag.

"Fifteen minutes, max," she responded after a quick glance on her phone. "I'll text you the info for the venue. I'll see you there," Sosie added before turning on her heels and marching away from Meredith's door.

Rushing back inside her room, Meredith pulled out the dress from the bag. Her jaw practically dropped to the ground as she stared at a gorgeous black gown. It looked simple, yet elegant. And she was confident she'd look stunning in it.

Aside from the gown, there were a couple of accessories inside the bag. But she settled for the simplest one – a black choker with an oval pendant that had a black crystal at the center.

A smile crept onto her mouth as excitement engulfed her. She thought that maybe this campaign wasn't so bad after all.

Stripping off her clothes, Meredith did her best to look presentable in the short amount of time she had. She'd had to skip a shower since there wasn't enough time, but she could at least wash her face and brush her teeth before applying fresh makeup.

She was determined to look her best.

Well, not really her *best* best – for now – since she didn't have a choice about what to wear. But at least she could try to make do with what she had.

After roughly ten minutes, she was surprised to find herself fully dressed and prepared as she stared at her reflection in the mirror.

Lily's going to freak out once she hears about this, she thought while grabbing her purse with the essentials in it – cellphone, credit cards and a bit of cash.

She had the concierge summon a cab for her. Checking the time on her phone, she was glad to hear the venue wasn't far from their hotel.

When the cab pulled over, she got off without hesitation, fully unaware that it was a red carpet event she'd be attending. Meredith shielded her face from the blinding camera flashes with her purse.

Just as she got used to the photographers, a limo pulled over in front of her.

She found herself breathless when Elijah emerged, leaving her speechless at how handsome he was. He looked like a panther in his black ensemble. His broad shoulders were apparent, as was his lean body.

She thought she'd look even better by his side, walking down the red carpet together.

But her fantasy immediately vanished when Sosie got down from the limo. She was wearing a burgundy satin gown, which looked amazing on her.

Right. How could she forget about the gorgeous campaign manager? As much as Meredith didn't want to think about it, she could sense that Sosie was definitely interested in Elijah. *Just like every other woman he meets*, she thought, rolling her eyes.

Clutching her purse, she took a deep breath and managed to crack a smile when the two noticed her presence. She would have turned and walked away already if she didn't think it would be inexcusably rude.

Until…

"Good evening, Meredith," Elijah greeted her, shooting her a huge grin. "Glad you made it," he added, looking her up and down admiringly.

She nodded when her eyes met his grey ones.

There was something in his stare that made her shudder in anticipation. Something that sent her messages of carnal awareness, like he found her to be the sexiest person alive.

Her stomach fluttered at the idea. An unfamiliar sensation engulfed her. It wasn't lust or happiness.

Instead, she was flattered.

She must have been crazy, but that's what she sensed.

Elijah Scott wanted her.

"Thank you for inviting me," she replied, trying her best to keep her expression polite and neutral.

Elijah beamed at her, and Sosie scowled.

But it didn't bother her one bit. She knew why Sosie was acting that way.

The two turned and made their way down the red carpet, leaving Meredith behind. But somehow, she didn't feel so out of place.

After all, she loved a good party.

$\mathcal{E}$li looked out over the crowd as he wrapped up the last few lines of his speech. Charity events such as this one weren't anything new, but he had to appear appropriately impressed, after all. He was virtually on autopilot, so he was mildly startled when the crowd broke into thunderous applause, and he quickly moved to step down from the podium.

Sosie immediately came and wrapped a hand around his upper arm, steering him toward a crowded table.

"Remember that we're here for donor support," she whispered under her breath as she smiled at a couple of middle-aged benefactors.

He sighed.

Eli hadn't grown up with this kind of wealth, and he certainly hadn't been raised in this kind of environment. But running for president meant he'd have to grin and bear it. It wasn't that he hated rich people. He just wasn't comfortable around them.

He shook hands with everyone Sosie introduced him to, made appropriate small talk, told jokes. But he couldn't remember the names of anyone he'd just met as his eyes constantly searched for Meredith.

He allowed himself to briefly fantasize about what it would be like to have Meredith as his date for an event like this. He suspected it would be fantastic. But he surprised himself by how much he wished that fantasy could become reality.

A few more minutes passed before he finally located her. She was fitting in quite well from the looks of things, looking completely at ease and in her element as she flitted around, chatting with various people. Of course the daughter of Benedict Fields would thrive in an environment like this. But he had never seen her wear her money like a mantle before, like these people.

Sosie led him to yet another table and introduced him to even more donors. He smiled and listened to their issues, promising their concerns would be his number one concerns if elected. Sosie expertly whisked him away just as the conversation started to lag.

"I think we can leave," Sosie whispered as a jazz band started playing in the background.

Eli smiled when he saw some of the guests get up on their feet and start to dance enthusiastically. He thought that maybe it wouldn't be so bad to stay and enjoy things a little bit longer.

"I want to stay and enjoy the drinks and music, I think," he mumbled.

He knew his campaign manager would be surprised. Inwardly he prepared to do battle, fully expecting her to argue with him and try to talk him out of the idea.

Sosie blinked.

"What?" she asked.

Eli understood where she was coming from. It was because she knew how much he found it uncomfortable to hang out with the rich crowd. And saying that he'd want to stay was a first.

"I'll stay," he repeated, gazing at Meredith again.

Following his stare, Sosie frowned.

"You shouldn't get involved with anyone. You know that," she reminded him.

He scowled. He knew that more than anyone else. She didn't need to tell him something he already knew.

"I know, Sosie."

She shrugged and checked her watch before sighing.

"I have three early morning interviews first thing tomor-row," she murmured.

"So go. I'll be fine," he replied, hoping he didn't sound rude.

"Don't do anything I wouldn't do," she warned again. "And don't stay out too late. You have a busy day tomorrow as well."

"Alright. I'll be back by midnight," he responded, and she nodded, evidently satisfied with that arrangement.

Who are you? Cinderella? Dude, get a life! a voice in his head mocked as he watched Sosie walk away.

Politely, he excused himself from the chitchat of the group around him, heading to where Meredith was – his eyes planted on her, afraid she might disappear if he took his eyes off her. She was talking with someone but when he approached them, the other woman politely excused herself and left the two of them alone.

He studied how lovely she looked with the way the gown accentuated her curvy body. She met his gaze when he edged closer to her. In her eyes was a glint of… he wasn't so sure. Surprise? Interest? Hunger?

But he thought he must have been imagining things.

"I see you made yourself comfortable," he commented.

"Yeah, well. I'm not sure why I'm here, so…" Meredith replied, shrugging.

Eli smirked.

"Dance with me," he said. It sounded like more of an order and less than an invitation. But as long as she agreed, he didn't really care how it came off.

Meredith cast a furtive glance around, looking to see if anyone had heard him. Her eyes were wide, and he found the expression on her face absolutely adorable.

"Are you sure that's a good idea?" she said hesitantly.

"I'm willing to take that chance," he whispered after taking her glass and setting it on a nearby table. "Come on," he urged, leading her to the dance floor, pulling her into his arms.

Eli felt her body tense as he slid his hands a few inches down her spine.

He was playing with fire, that was for sure.

He was undeniably attracted to her.

Leading the dance, he got a whiff of her perfume. It smelled like mild vanilla with the hint of something spicier underneath.

How appropriate, he thought.

Meredith's movements were stiff, and she avoided his gaze as they danced. Maybe some small talk would help her relax.

"So, how are you liking the job so far? Is it everything you hoped it would be?"

Eli felt her hands tense on his shoulders as she glanced at him, shaking her head.

"Nope. And I didn't have my choice of assignments," she stated flatly.

"You do know that this is a very sought after assignment, right?" he asked, cocking an eyebrow at her.

"What? Being on a bus all day with a bunch of people I don't know? I could do that anywhere," she retorted with a frown.

"You're with the best of the best. I bet if you ask around, you'll find out that your rivals are quite well prepared for the task. I imagine some of them even fought to get the position. And yet, you seem to feel like your time could be better spent elsewhere."

Meredith smiled impishly, melting his insides. He could feel his stomach twisting as his heart pounded against his ribcage. How did she fucking do that?

"It's not that, exactly. It's just… you know, my best friend is partying in Bali, going to huge ragers on yachts. And I'm… here," she explained with a shrug.

"Did you even study journalism in school?" he questioned sarcastically, earning himself an offended look.

"I'll have you know that I graduated at the top of my class. I just thought… I thought my concentration would be elsewhere."

"Like going to parties on yachts?" he said teasingly.

He grinned. It was gone in an instant, but he noticed her looking at his mouth.

"I thought I'd concentrate on fashion, maybe. Or music…"

"Ah, I see. So the presidential race just isn't exciting enough for you," he noted.

She looked at him with a serious expression, meeting his eyes with her deep blues.

"Why are you so interested in me?" she questioned.

Eli chuckled in amusement. "It's not every day that I run into the sexy stranger who gave me the lap dance of my life. You're the only woman who's been able to capture my attention for more than a fleeting instant. Why shouldn't I be interested?" he spoke huskily, maintaining eye contact. "Because you have a campaign to run?" she replied contemptuously.

He laughed softly.

"No, Sosie has a campaign to run. I just show up where she tells me to," he mumbled, half to himself.

Meredith smirked at him like he had misspoke.

"Well, then I guess you shouldn't be interested in me because I'm twenty-three, and you're... what, thirty-six? Thirty-seven?" she said.

Eli winced upon the mention of their considerable age difference.

"Thirty-five," he supplied. "My birthday is in January."

Meredith sighed heavily. "If anyone sees you making a move on me, it'll create trouble. And trouble is something that a presidential candidate does not need."

"Touché," he replied.

She stopped dancing and pulled away from his grasp, looking at him with a blank expression on her face. He didn't know how to react.

"So let me go," she stated firmly in a low and very stern voice.

"Just give me until the end of this song," he found himself begging.

But instead of saying anything, Meredith shot him a meaningful look and broke free from his hold. She walked away gracefully, and there was nothing he could do as she left.

Damn. He needed to get a hold of himself.

12

After two weeks on the road, Meredith found herself back in D.C. She'd planned on spending her limited downtime relaxing, but instead she was roped into making an appearance at a party her parents had thrown. Her mother's friends had been asking her about marriage, and that was the last thing she wanted to think about.

Well, maybe the second to last thing she wanted to think about. Elijah Scott was actually the last thing she wanted to think about, as much as it pained her to admit that. She tried not to scowl when Mason, a guy she'd known in high school, approached her with a wide grin on his face.

He kissed her hand, and she resisted the urge to wipe it off on her dress.

"Lovely seeing you again, Mer," he said.

Mason was gorgeous. With an Italian father and Russian mother, his good looks had ensured he'd never wanted for a date their entire time together in high school. *He cleaned up nicely, too*, she thought, looking at how he filled out his designer tux.

"Hi, Mason. It's good to see you, too," she replied coolly.

She didn't have anything against Mason per se. She just hated the idea of their parents conspiring to marry them off. She was well aware people had always assumed they'd end up together someday. Which was ridiculous, because they'd never gone on a date together, not even once.

Like her, Mason McGuire was practically American royalty. He was the heir to MG Holdings, the largest electric company in the country. His family's wealth rivaled that of hers. But she didn't care about any of that.

Mason McGuire held about as much attraction for her as a damp sponge. There was just something about his personality she'd always found off-putting.

"Would you care for a dance?" he asked.

She wanted to roll her eyes as she stared at his outstretched arm. As if she could possibly turn him down when he knew damn well both sets of their parents were watching them like hawks.

"Sure," she said, plastering a huge fake smile on her face before setting her champagne flute down.

When they got to the dance floor, Mason pulled her close with his hands wrapped around her waist. She felt really awkward in his arms.

"Our parents are practically planning our wedding," he whispered in her ear.

Meredith tensed. She didn't know how to respond without sounding rude and conceited. She knew Mason had his pick of women. But she wasn't sure if he liked the idea of marrying for business and not love.She fervently hoped he was against it.

"I know," she responded simply.

"So, what do you think about it?" he asked, his grasp on her waist tightening.

"What do *you* think about it?" she asked, staring into his chocolate brown eyes that seemed to be always smiling. Eyes that didn't do a damn thing for her. Not like a certain someone's grey eyes...

"I asked you first."

She shrugged.

"I don't know. I haven't given it a lot of thought. You know... I still have a lot of things I want to do," she murmured hopefully.

Mason smiled.

"Like?" he urged.

"Like enjoying the single life?" she asked sarcastically, earning herself a soft chuckle.

"Your reason should be more compelling than that. You know, to make it sound more convincing," he teased with a smirk, exposing his deep dimples. "You like someone else, don't you?"

She tensed. Did she?

As much as she wanted to deny it, she knew she was doomed.

Yes, she liked Elijah Scott. Like, a lot.

Like, *a lot* a lot.

But being together with him would be impossible.

"Yes," she admitted, feeling a lump in her throat.

His smirk turned into a wide grin.

"I see."

After that, Mason thankfully remained silent. He led her back to the table where she'd left her champagne and kissed her hand once more before saying goodbye. Looking in his eyes, she thought she saw a glint of regret. But she was probably just imagining things.

Mason had never expressed any serious interest in her in all the years she'd known him.

The moment Meredith settled back into her seat, she soon felt a nudge on her side. It was her little sister, Bonnie.

If Meredith was her mother's carbon copy, Bonnie took after their father. Her hair was dark, as were her eyes.

"What did you talk about?" Bonnie asked.

She shrugged. "Nothing."

"Don't lie to me, Mer. I saw you two," her younger sister replied, rolling her eyes. "Now, come on. Spill the beans."

Grabbing a crystal goblet filled with water on her right, she took a few sips to alleviate the sudden dryness of her throat. She was still surprised by how the conversation with Mason had gone.

"We talked about marriage," she said dryly, looking across the room. It looked like their parents were having a cozy chat with the McGuires.

"What?!" Bonnie shrieked. "Are you saying that Mason McGuire is going to be my brother-in-law?" Meredith fought back the urge to chuckle when she saw the distressed look on Bonnie's face.

Bonnie had liked Mason for years. Meredith had assumed it was nothing more than a crush that Bonnie would eventually grow out of, but now she wasn't so sure judging by the bitter glare her sister was giving her. Bonnie was nineteen, so there was only a four year difference between her and Mason.

Her eyes widened when an idea crossed her mind.

"Why don't you marry him?" she suggested.

"If only," Bonnie huffed, lightly stomping her feet under the table.

A moment of silence passed, but when their eyes met they giggled playfully. They watched as their parents approached their table.

"Tell them," her sister whispered, nudging her.

"You're still nineteen, Bonnie. Let's wait until you turn twenty-one, okay?" She added, "Don't you want to be able to drink and celebrate the toasts at your own wedding?"

"Whatever.," the latter said stubbornly with a smile.

"Enjoying the night so far, girls?" Benedict Fields asked.

Meredith and Bonnie nodded their heads in response. Their mom eyed them suspiciously, but chose not to say a word.

Her parents turned away momentarily to greet more guests, but soon came back over to their table.

"May I please be excused? I haven't gotten much sleep lately while I've been on the road with the campaign," Meredith said.

"Me too," Bonnie stated.

"Bonnie, you too?" her father said with a slight frown.

"Please," they chorused.

Their mom smiled.

"Just let them be, Benedict. They won't be seeing each other often for the next few months," Elizabeth pointed out, then smiled and nodded at the guests that passed by their table.

"Alright, alright."

It didn't take long for Meredith and Bonnie to get ready for bed. Bonnie joined her in her room, something she'd done since she was a little girl and they'd held sleepover parties with just the two of them. They giggled and gossiped as they got caught up on what had been happening in each other's lives.

Bonnie soon passed out on Meredith's bed, and as she draped a soft cashmere throw over her slumbering sister, she realized that for the first time, she was truly glad she'd decided to accept her dad's offer for the summer. She really loved her little sister, and she was grateful to spend some time with her, brief as it was. Careful not to wake Bonnie up as she climbed into bed next to her, she soon fell into a dark, dreamless sleep.

13

*E*li held a pool party at his place the day before he was scheduled to get back on the road for the campaign. All of his staff was invited, including his traveling press pool... and Meredith.

It was a decidedly casual affair. He wanted a chance to unwind and relax, and he hoped his guests would share this sentiment.

Looking at the crowd gathered by the pool, Eli searched for the one person he wanted to see. But it looked like Meredith hadn't yet arrived. If she was even coming to his party.

"Looking for someone?" Sosie asked.

She looked stunning in a yellow sundress. Eli had to admit she was gorgeous. And he was aware she had a thing for him.

He suspected it was her romantic feelings for him that had prompted her to volunteer to run his campaign.

And Eli was sincerely thankful for that.

But he didn't think he'd ever be able to return her feelings, as much as he wished he could sometimes. Then maybe things wouldn't seem so complicated.

"Nope," he said, walking away before she could respond. He headed across the patio to where a large folding table had been set up to hold various party snacks and finger foods.

He poured himself a drink and stood next to the table, sipping at his whisky and tapping his foot impatiently against the ground. The party had started over thirty minutes ago, and Meredith still hadn't arrived.

Where the hell is she?

Eli didn't know why he was so eager to see Meredith. He'd just seen her two days ago when they'd returned to D.C. for the weekend. Those days had felt like months though.

He missed her.

"Pining for some jailbait is not a good look," he heard Sosie practically snarl at his side.

Yes, he knew that Sosie was only looking out for him – and his political career. But there were times when he wanted to snap at her and tell her to mind her own business. Times like right now, for instance.

"I'm not pining for anyone," he replied, smiling at Ava as she walked past them.

"I'm just reminding you to be careful," Sosie murmured, tugging firmly at his sleeve.

"I already know that, Sosie. I'll be fine. Now go have fun," he said, shooing her away to avoid prolonging the conversation.

"Alright. Alright," she grumbled, walking away from him, joining the group of women sitting by the pool who were soaking their feet in the water.

A few moments later, Eli headed inside. He didn't want to ruin the party for everyone else just because he was in a bad mood. He heard one of his favorite songs come on as he was washing his hands.

At least there's one thing I can enjoy about this stupid party, he thought, singing along with the song at the top of his lungs while he looked at his reflection in the mirror. That seemed to do the trick.

Feeling a little better, he went back to the pool to accommodate his guests. He needed to be a good host instead of feeling sorry for himself.

Looking around, he saw Meredith chatting with Ava and some other people. She looked stunning in a dark denim dress and flats. Her hair was arranged into a messy bun with wispy strands surrounding her face, and she had worn minimal makeup. He found the whole look incredibly attractive.

Hanging back so she wouldn't see him, he continued to study her. He was captivated by all her mannerisms and quirks.

He watched as she licked at her luscious lips, and though it wasn't a sexual gesture, his thoughts quickly turned sexual in nature. He imagined how it would feel to fuck her in the pool, the water warm and only adding to their mutual pleasure.

"Eli!" he heard a familiar voice say behind him, jolting him out of his fantasy, back to reality. Familiar, but completely unexpected.

He turned to greet his younger brother, Ryan Scott.

"Ryan? What are you doing here?" he asked, embracing his brother in a tight hug. Now this was a pleasant surprise, but also a much-needed distraction.

Eli hadn't expected to see his brother at all this year. A decorated officer on active duty, Ryan Scott was rarely home for more than few days at a time. They'd barely seen each other since Eli had gone into politics, and his brother had joined the military.

"I'd tell you, but then I'd have to kill you," his brother said with a wink as they shared a laugh. The joke never got old, and Eli knew there was probably a hint of truth to the statement.

"I'm gonna grab a drink," Ryan said. "Be right back."

Eli watched as his younger brother approached the table to get a drink. And he found himself holding his breath when Meredith accidentally bumped into him. She looked quite taken aback when she looked at Ryan.

Not that he was particularly surprised by her reaction.

Ryan looked like a younger version of him. They had the same frame, but Ryan was a few inches shorter than Eli. When they were kids, they were often mistaken for twins.

His hands balled into fists when they continued to talk even after Ryan had finished pouring himself a drink. Not that he thought Meredith was encouraging his brother or anything like that. But he knew Ryan was a goddamn player when it came to women. And Meredith was obviously his next target.

Eli watched them as they moved to the edge of the pool, growing increasingly jealous. He heard Meredith laugh at something Ryan had whispered, and suddenly he was seeing red. Seeing her happy and smiling because of someone else made him unreasonably angry. What was worse was that it wasn't some stranger making her laugh. It was his brother.

He wasn't sure how long Ryan had been flirting with her before she headed inside the house. Eli followed her indoors, and waited for her to finish up using the bathroom.

He was furious, and he knew he had no right to be. It wasn't like they were even together. But he didn't care. All he knew was that he couldn't let her end up with his brother.

When she exited the bathroom, he grabbed her by the wrist, making her gasp in surprise. "Eli? What are you doing?" she asked.

Without bothering to reply, he dragged her down the hallway to the laundry room and shut the door, making sure they would be alone. She angrily jerked out of his grasp.

"What are you —"

He pulled her close and planted a savage kiss on her lips. It was neither soft nor sweet. He continued to devour her mouth ruthlessly, punishing her for making him feel this way.

He could feel her struggling in his arms, doing her best to pull away. That just made him angrier. He kissed her even harder, not stopping until he tasted blood.

Had he gone too far?

Meredith immediately slapped him hard on the face, looking at him with disgust and anger. His eyes widened when he noticed her eyes shining with unshed tears.

Fuck. What the hell was the matter with him?

Eli wanted to kick his own ass when his eyes landed on her mouth. Her lips were bleeding and swollen. He'd hurt her.

He hadn't meant to.

And it hadn't been his intention to upset her.

"Let's just forget this happened," she said, wiping at her mouth.

"Why? I enjoyed it," he said angrily. He swore he could see steam coming out from his nostrils.

"Well, I didn't," she fired back immediately, eyes bulging in anger.

"I suppose you'd say otherwise if it had been Ryan," he sneered.

"What —"

"Stop flirting with my brother, Miss Fields. You want to play? I'm up for it anytime. But leave my brother out of this."

With that he stormed out of the room, slamming the door hard behind him. He wasn't sure if his words made any sense, but at that moment, he didn't care. All he knew was that he wanted to make it clear to her that he wasn't happy.

He let out a deep sigh when he reached his bedroom. He'd hang out here for a few minutes and compose himself, so none of his guests would see him acting like a neanderthal. But what was wrong with him? He had no right to be this upset. And what was wrong with Ryan making a move on her?

You're just jealous because you know they could have a shot at a real relationship, unlike you and Meredith.

Jealous?

Gritting his teeth, Eli examined his reflection in the mirror. He closed his eyes and cracked his neck, hoping to relieve some of the tension he was feeling.

He opened his eyes after a few moments, then sighed.

Yes, he was jealous.

14

Meredith found herself at yet another charity fundraiser. This time, they were in Seattle. And this time, she was Elijah's date, not just a replacement for someone in his entourage.

She'd grudgingly accepted his invitation even though she was still offended by their last encounter. He'd dragged her away like a caveman, then kissed her against her will – she ignored the voice in the back of her head slyly whispering that kissing Elijah was exactly what she'd wanted – and then he'd had the nerve to accuse her of flirting with his brother, when she'd just been trying to be friendly.

But he genuinely seemed remorseful, and he'd begged her for the chance to apologize and make things up to her. She wanted to give him a chance to redeem himself, she supposed.

"Good evening Elijah," said a middle-aged woman as she shook hands with him. She eyed Meredith curiously.

"It's good to see you, Marge," Elijah replied with a smile.

"And who might this beautiful woman be?" Marge asked, referring to her.

Meredith swallowed. Here was the moment of truth. She wasn't sure how he'd planned on introducing her to the people at tonight's event.

"This is Meredith Fields. She's my date," Elijah replied proudly, looking at her like she was the most beautiful person in the room.

She felt immensely flattered.

But she also felt a chilly gaze from across the room, like someone was dragging the point of a dagger down her spine. And she wasn't far from the mark.. Across the room, Sosie was watching them, looking evidently displeased with the way Elijah had brought her to the party.

"Date?" Marge asked suspiciously. "Or dating?"

Elijah only chuckled and shook his head politely, shrugging off the question.

Meredith took her seat at the table closest to the stage as Elijah began his speech. It was the same speech she'd heard several times throughout the campaign, but his charisma still made everything seem fresh. His poise and authority were undeniable.

As expected from a president-to-be.

After the speech and a short, obviously heated conversation with a fuming Sosie, and even though Meredith was hardly able to take her eyes off of him, Elijah was still able to sneak up on her.

"How was it?" Elijah whispered..

They chatted with donors for about an hour until Elijah gripped her wrist, sneaking their way out of the ballroom.

"What are you doing?" she hissed, looking around to make sure nobody was watching them. Despite her reservations, she felt a thrill of excitement to be sneaking around with Eli.

"Taking you somewhere quiet and lovely. Or maybe just taking someone lovely somewhere quiet."

Following his lead, they went upstairs and ended up in the balcony. Meredith gasped as she looked at the breathtaking view of the city. The lights looked like stars glittering on land.

Did that make any sense? She didn't know. All she knew was that she had never found the dark all that beautiful until now.

They shared a comfortable silence as for a couple of minutes until she decided not to waste the opportunity to get to know him better now that they were alone with a million glittering lights.

"Aside from becoming president, what are your goals in life?" she asked, looking gazing out across the city. "Ten years from now, where do you see yourself?"

She expected a polished, yet generic response for such a trite question. When he didn't answer her, she tilted her head to look at his face. His expression was not what she'd expected. Eli looked surprised.

"What is it?" she said, and his expression softened.

He gave her a sad smile, then shrugged.

"No one's ever asked me that before," he explained.

"I was just curious," she said quietly, looking back out across the city. She hadn't meant to make him sad. After a moment he cleared his throat.

"I guess... I don't know where I see myself," he admitted reluctantly. "Right now, it's hard to see beyond the presidency. Hell, it's hard to see past November third."

"Sure, that's understandable. But what about before you decided to run for president? You really didn't have anything in mind?" she asked. Maybe if she rephrased the question she'd get a better answer.

He grinned.

"Off the record?" he asked.

"If you want, sure."

"I'd just gotten out of the Navy when I started thinking about running for office. I had a very specific idea of what I thought the ideal presidential candidate should be. Single," he said with a wry smile, "was not part of that equation. So I dated several women who each would have been the perfect political partner. Even got close to proposing to one of them – Rachel. But I asked myself, 'Why am I marrying her?' Just like the others, she didn't make me happy. She just made me a stronger candidate.

Meredith laughed as Elijah's expression shifted from confusion, to relief and maybe – if she was right – a bit of regret.

"So what happened?" she prompted, curious about what had happened between him and Rachel.

"I pulled back, got some much-needed perspective. I realized I wanted to earn the presidency through my own merits, not because I was part of some glitzy power couple. And I guess I realized marriage is a serious commitment. And I just wasn't that serious about Rachel, or any of the other women I'd dated."

His last sentence made her smile wider than it probably should have. But still, she was pleased to confirm he'd rather be single than to marry for personal gain, and not love.

"Your turn, Meredith. Where do you see yourself ten years from now?" he asked.

"I thought I had things all figured out," she said. "But now I'm not so sure," she said with a frown.

"Oh? Do tell, Miss Fields," Eli said, and she rolled her eyes.

"I guess I always thought I'd have a job at a top fashion magazine, and then maybe I'd get married for money, not for love. My parents' friends have a son who's my age."

Eli raised a brow, not the least bit shocked.

"Really?"

"Yeah. I mean… my mom's friends ask me when I'm going to settle down and stuff like that, or when I'm going to get my 'MRS' degree.".

She was expecting Elijah to at least smile but he didn't. Instead, his jaws clenched and his muscles tensed. She was not even sure if it was right to feel happy about it.

"Anyone particular caught your eye?" he asked.

"For marriage?" She shook her head. I don't think so."

They slipped back into a comfortable silence again, and Meredith's heart felt full.. Was it because the night view was beautiful? Was it because she felt good? Or was it because she was with the man who had been challenging her ever since he came crashing in her life?

She didn't know.

But whatever it was, she hoped tonight would never end.

He broke the silence. "Are you dating anyone seriously?"

"What? Like a boyfriend? Are you seriously asking if I have a boyfriend?" she asked wide-eyed, angry at the question for taking her out of a perfectly cozy moment..

"I'm just asking," he replied, his grey eyes drilling into her.

Meredith's heart skipped a beat and her stomach twisted into a knot when Elijah pulled her close with his arm around her waist.

His breath was heavy as it brushed her face. And he smelled so fucking good – a mixture of mint, aftershave and bit of his natural masculine scent. His eyes melted her and it was taking her breath away. How could he possibly have such an affect on her?

She closed her eyes and her hands on his shoulders turned into fists when he pulled her even closer. Something magical was about to happen. She didn't know how much she missed having his lips on hers until now.

God, she missed his kisses. She missed getting a taste of him.

She missed *him*.

You're crazy, she thought when she felt him inching ever closer.

But she didn't care.

Everything that had been happening to her ever since the night of the party was crazy. Insane might be a better word for it. And it was all because of the man who was just about to kiss her.

She closed her eyes and raised her lips to meet him.

And suddenly a loud, irritated cough made her open her eyes, and pull away from Elijah like something had burned her.

Sosie had found them, and was dragging Elijah away without saying a word to Meredith.

"What are you doing here? I've been looking all over for you! And here you are, with her..." The venom in her voice was apparent even as her words faded into the distance as the door shut behind her.

With a heavy sigh, Meredith turned to look out over the city once more. A million shining lights looked up at her in consolation, but she couldn't help feeling like someone had turned off her switch.

"Mmmm..." Elijah moaned.

He didn't know if he was having another dream. But he was fucking horny and whatever he was feeling seemed too real.

"Hmph… Hmph…" he heard a muffled voice from under the sheets. And he grunted in pleasure at the feeling of a cool hand wrapping around his burning cock..

With a giggle that seemed to voice the delight he was feeling, a blonde woman came out of the sheets, searing his mouth with a kiss like a hungry beast.

It was Meredith.

She was completely naked. Her full breasts rubbed against his chest. He didn't know how she ended up in his room since the last thing he remembered was masturbating in an empty room as he imagined her sucking his cock..

With intense lust, he responded to her kisses and let his hands roam under the sheets, taking two handfuls of her ass... He was too fucking horny to think straight and all he knew was that he needed release. He gripped her wrist, leading her hands back to his erection – to touch him, feel him and pleasure him.

He sucked a ragged breath through clenched teeth as her nimble fingers wrapped around his hard member.

"I know," she whispered against his lips, stroking his erection very slowly, teasing him.

He grunted in bliss, lost in the ocean of her blue eyes.

Eli had fucked a lot of women before. But this was the very first time he had allowed someone to take control over him.. And it was effortless for her. For all of his walls, a single touch from her was like a wrecking ball. With her, he was defenseless.

It was serious.

But he loved the way she moved against him, driving him absolutely insane in a way no one else had ever done.

He gathered her in his arms, kissing her hard, not wasting a second. He needed to taste her. She moaned into his mouth when he nibbled her lower lip, her body aching for more.

Her hand moved rhythmically caressing his cock very carefully, almost gently, sending chills down his spine and pushing him to the brink of insanity. He thrust his hips against her hand.

God, he fucking loved what she was doing!

But she stopped.

Elijah made a protesting growl which faded into a groan when Meredith went under the sheets, positioned her small figure in between his legs, and swallowed his erection almost to the hilt..

"Yeah… Jesus! Meredith!" he exclaimed as her mouth adjusted to his length. She continued teasing him, her tongue moved around the swollen head of his penis, licking him like a lollipop. And that was when he realized that it's not easy to be the one to give up control.

"You taste so good, Elijah," she mumbled, savoring a bead of precum as it snaked down his shaft.

He chuckled.

"I'll take your word for it," he said, removing the thin sheets that covered her to get a better of view of her curvaceous body before wrapping her blonde hair around his fist and pulling it away from her face.

He took a good look at her swaying breasts as she continued fucking him with her mouth. It was a beautiful sight.

She was a fucking sex goddess. And he would never get tired of looking at her like this – her naked and sucking him like a piece of candy.

When she started licking his balls, his eyes rolled back and he , shuddered in excitement. With all his remaining strength, he pulled her up so that she was straddling him. Her legs were stretched wide apart and his cock slid between the wet lips of her pussy..

He pulled her close enough to share breath, sliding his hips ever so slightly to the left and right, so the roundness of his cock would press against her clit.

"And now for your punishment," he whispered into her mouth, before rolling her over and pinning her down underneath him. His cock rubbed against the smooth skin of her belly as his mouth found her breasts.

Meredith moaned in response..

"You're so fucking sexy, Meredith," he whispered as his tongue pressed her left nipple against his teeth. He gently rolled the other between his fingers..

He took his time teasing her as he moved the wet tip of his cock to rest against her even wetter entrance, making them both gasp for air. It was fleeting, yet the beating of his heart matched the rhythm of her breathing.

Her hands reached out for him, and she unconsciously moved her hips to take him inside. But for each of her maneuvers, Elijah had a counter-maneuver, keeping them ever on the edge of sex. .She was getting impatient. And nobody would ever think that the prim and proper Meredith Fields was naughty in bed.

He loved the idea that only he could see that side of her.

As the eagerness to have her grew stronger, Elijah trailed kisses from her mouth down to her belly, stopping just an inch before her wet folds. He earned a protesting moan.

He wanted her to say his name.

He wanted her to beg for his cock.

Slowly, his tongue traveled to her dripping pussy, tasting her desire. He smiled, finally able to find the words to describe her flavor. She tasted like a mixture of minerals and sweetness of honey. And he loved it.

He swirled his tongue on her most sensitive spot.

"Ohhh… Ahhh… Hmmm…" she moaned. Every muscle in his body was screaming for her flesh.

Getting impatient himself, he sucked her wet pussy as she arched her body to signal that she wanted more. And without further foreplay, he positioned in between her parted thighs, easing and probing his cock into her cunt.

In a single thrust, he filled her with his length. And the feeling of her muscles tightening around him drove him mad. Only when she had adjusted to his size did he begin to move. . His thrusts were slow at first. Then he picked up his pace, pounding her, eager to hear more of her screams.

"Oh! Oh! Damn! Yes!" she exclaimed as sweat trickled down her face.

He cupped her breasts and kissed her hard, moving faster, almost reaching his climax.

"I can't hear you," he spoke heavily.

"Jesus! Just fuck me, Elijah!" she screamed in between heavy panting, moving her body to meet his thrusts, her carnal muscles tightening around this throbbing cock as he sucked and kissed her breasts.

His breathing had grown erratic, and hers was hot as he went faster and deeper. With one last thrust, he shot his load inside her.

Elijah woke up covered in sweat, his heart racing so hard he thought it might escape from his chest. Yet again, he was almost painfully hard.

Of course it was too good to be true, he thought, shaking his head. He got out of bed and headed straight for the bathroom.

Just like every night since Seattle, he'd had a sex dream starring Meredith. The dreams kept getting more realistic, leaving him frustrated beyond belief upon waking. He knew he'd be unable to concentrate or get anything done if he didn't take care of himself, so he stroked his cock in the shower – just as he'd done every morning since Seattle.

Elijah was starting to think it was going to turn into a permanent routine at this rate.

After his shower, he got dressed in his favorite pair of pajamas and decided to relax on the sofa with a can of beer, maybe catch a game if any of his teams were playing. Before he could crack open his beer, he heard a knock at his door.

He frowned. He hadn't been expecting anyone. He had no idea who it could be.

He opened the door to find Sosie standing there in a silk robe that was so thin, it left almost nothing to the imagination.

"Sosie?" he said, startled. She smiled.

"Surprise!" she said, letting out a harsh, grating laugh. She reeked of alcohol. Was she drunk?

"Let me in," she demanded, forcing her way into his suite and sweeping past him before he could stop her. She stumbled after a few steps, and he caught her just in time.

"Careful," he muttered, helping her toward the sofa. This wasn't like Sosie at all.

Sosie smiled as he sat her down, and reached out to caress his face.

"Elijah, Elijah," she whispered softly. Her robe had slipped open, though it seemed she hadn't noticed.

Gritting his teeth, he averted his gaze.

"I'll make some coffee. You need to sober up," he said. But Sosie grabbed him by the wrists, and pulled him down onto the sofa with her.

"No, stay," she murmured, straddling his lap.

Elijah didn't know how to respond when she started kissing him hungrily. He considered her nothing more than a good friend. But it was clear she wanted more.

He knew sleeping with her would just complicate things more.

But a tiny part of him said he should give things a shot with her. That it would be better than being with Meredith. Sosie was only two years younger than him, and had always been driven and ambitious. She would make a good partner for him.

She moaned sexily against his mouth.

The sound reminded him of the dreams he'd been having about Meredith. His thoughts always came back to her, even with another woman on top of him.

When Sosie's hand reached down to lightly brush against his cock, he realized he couldn't go through with this. This wasn't what he wanted.

This is wrong, he thought. And taking advantage of the situation would hardly be fair to Sosie.

He pushed Sosie off of his lap and moved to the other end of the sofa, putting some distance between them. Judging by her expression, she was pissed.

"This is wrong, Sosie. I'm sorry. I can't."

Sosie scoffed in disbelief.

"Are you fucking kidding me? You're turning me down?" she growled angrily.

She stood up abruptly, drawing her robe tight around her and tying the sash at her waist.

Elijah stood up. "We can talk tomorrow. Go back to your room and get some sleep." Part of him felt slightly idiotic for passing on Sosie.

"Unbelievable," Sosie muttered under her breath, storming out of his room.

What the hell is happening to me? he thought, looking at his throbbing cock, cursing as he started stroking himself once more.

He stared at the ceiling. When would he be able to get a dose of sex that he badly needed? And hopefully, with someone whom he liked?

Like Meredith?

He groaned as he picked up the pace.

The whole situation was driving him insane.

He'd never thought his life could be this complicated!

16

*M*eredith, along with some of the other reporters, decided to go clubbing to take their minds off of work for a night. As the summer progressed, she'd grown comfortable with most everyone. She'd even made friends with a few. Sosie remained aloof, but she guessed that couldn't be helped.

Meredith had agonized over what to wear, finally deciding upon a violet minidress and nude heels. At first she'd worried it was overly revealing, but it covered more than the blue dress she'd been wearing at the masquerade party, so she decided to just go with it.

When they reached the club, Meredith felt completely at ease for the first time since she'd started this assignment.

For a moment, it was easy to pretend like this was just another night in the city and she was partying with Lily.

She dragged Ava over to the bar. After a few shots of vodka, Meredith was feeling good and more than ready to dance. When a stranger pressed up against her from behind, she went with the flow, grinding seductively on him.

She spun around, wanting to see who she was dancing with, and she felt like someone had thrown a glass of water in her face when she saw none other than Mason.

She pulled him away from the dance floor, back toward the bar. Mason was the last person she'd expected to see.

"Meredith, relax," Mason said as they found some seats. She frowned.

"What are you doing here?" she asked.

Mason watched her intently.

"What would you do if I said I followed you here?" he asked, deadly serious.

"Wha– I don't– Why–" she mumbled, unable to compose a proper sentence.

Mason laughed, and she blushed furiously. She should have known he wasn't serious.

"I'm just kidding. I was here a couple of days ago for a business meeting. And well… here I am," he said mischievously, studying her figure, his eyes full of admiration – and lust.

"Fine," she answered back, rolling her eyes when she felt his gaze landing on her cleavage. "My colleagues are waiting for me," she added.

"They'll be fine," Mason said, gripping her wrist when she rose from her seat. It wasn't tight, but it was enough to stop her.

She shot him a dirty look, but he was undeterred. Scowling, she jerked out of his grasp and settled back into her seat. She suspected he was up to something, but she wasn't sure what.

"What are you really doing here? Spill it, Mason," she commanded.

He smiled faintly.

"Fine. I surrender. You win," he said.

Instead of saying anything, Meredith merely crossed her arms over her chest and eyed him warily.

"I've decided. We're going to get married. And so I'm here to make sure you're the person I want to spend the rest of my life with," he stated confidently.

He'd decided? As if her own feelings weren't a factor at all? She didn't know whether to laugh or feel insulted.

"Are you drunk?" she asked in disbelief.

"Of course not!" he snapped. But despite the dim lighting, she could tell he was blushing.

Meredith giggled, realizing he was serious.

"I know I don't sound like the Mason McGuire you know, okay? But I'm serious. I've dated a lot of girls–"

"Fucked," she interrupted, correcting his choice of word.

"Whatever," he answered, rolling his eyes. "But that's not the point. We're talking about marriage here, Mer. I don't want to get married with someone just for business."

"Oh, we actually agree on something for once," she said sarcastically.

"I just… you know," he grumbled.

"What?"

"I want to fall in love, too."

That simple confession was enough to make her burst into laughter. She wasn't sure why it was so hilarious. Maybe because it was Mason who said it. She'd never expected to have this kind of conversation with him.

"Stop laughing," he said, evidently annoyed.

"Did you come all the way here just to tell me that?" she asked, eyes wide as the thought occurred to her. "I'm sorry for laughing, but you have to admit it's hilarious. You, talking about falling in love?"

"I came here to tell you that I don't have any plans to marry you," he stated angrily.

Meredith smiled. That was the best news she'd heard in a long time.

With that settled, they spent some time catching up in between doing shots. Sure, there was zero romantic attraction between them, but they'd known each other since they were teenagers, and they had plenty in common otherwise. Mason confessed that he was still unsure of his path in life beyond inheriting his family's company, which made her feel better about her own situation. At least she was striving toward the life she really wanted.

"Come on, let's have some fun!" Mason said, leading her back out onto the dance floor.

It was almost midnight.

Meredith danced like there was no tomorrow. But she wished Elijah were keeping her company instead.

Who am I kidding? He's not going to show up. He doesn't have time to have a little fun, she thought.

Her heart sank a little.

Even now, Elijah was the only person she wanted to dance with.

But it looked as though it would merely remain just one of her fantasies.

17

Meredith marched into the hotel lobby, swaying unsteadily on her feet. She'd left the club after she realized she wasn't really enjoying it anymore. She couldn't stop obsessing over Elijah, and her colleagues had been nowhere to be found. Maybe they'd all found people to hook up with, unlike her.

Good for them, she thought, pressing the button for the elevator.

Her dress might have been skimpy, but she felt flushed, almost feverish. Taking a cold shower was definitely in order once she got back to her room. Her lip curled with disdain when she realized that even a cold shower probably wouldn't drive the thoughts of Elijah from her mind. Pathetic.

She got off the elevator when it reached her floor. Just as she passed by Elijah's room, she saw him approach. He was in gym clothes, and he looked like he'd just come back from working out.

She swallowed hard, then licked her lips.

She thought she'd give anything just to lick that sweat off his body as her eyes traveled to his arms, down to his strong legs, then to the bulge in between his legs. Damn! Once again, the alcohol had made her bold.

"Hi!" she greeted, hoping she didn't look like a hot mess.

"Meredith," he uttered sensuously, looking her up and down.

"I was waiting for you tonight, didn't you know?" she blurted suddenly. It wasn't a complete lie, considering how she'd kept obsessively checking for him at the club.

"What?" Elijah said, surprised.

"I was waiting for you," she repeated, this time more flirtatiously. She nibbled his earlobe and closed her eyes when she realized she liked the salty taste of his sweat.

She smiled when she felt him shudder, and his muscles tensed when she squirmed against his strong body.

"Why?" he asked, his hands moving to her waist.

"Because I missed you?" she answered mischievously in his ear.

Elijah pushed her away abruptly.

"Come on, I'll walk you to your room. You need to get some rest. You're drunk," he said angrily.

"No!" she said stubbornly.

"What are you doing?" he hissed when she started planting tiny kisses on his neck.

God, she would never have had the courage to make a move if she was sober.

Elijah looked around, afraid that people might see them. After a moment though, he opened the door to his room, bringing Meredith inside with him.

When she heard the door click shut behind them, she kissed him on the lips without warning.

Not knowing what she was doing, she pulled him closer.

"Mmmm…" she moaned when his hands found her breasts, releasing them from the restraints of the tight dress, cupping them hard.

Meredith didn't know if she was seducing him, or the other way around. But she decided she didn't care. She was powerless to resist him.

She'd wanted him ever since the first time they met.

Her body ached for him.

Elijah was the only man who'd ever made her feel this way.

He scooped her up and laid her on the bed. She realized her dress was on the floor.

She shivered in embarrassment and excitement. This was the first time someone had stripped her of her clothes.

The first time someone had seen her in just her underwear.

Meredith shyly covered herself up with the comforter as Elijah stood in front of her, slowly removing his clothes.

Just as she had suspected, Elijah looked like an underwear model. Tanned and muscular, he looked even better in person than she could have ever imagined.

She gulped as her attention was focused on the heavy bulge under his boxers.

He knelt down to finally remove his remaining garment. All she could do was stare at his fullness. She cursed quietly and swallowed hard when she saw his glorious erection.

He was beautiful.

Meredith had never seen anything like it before. His cock was long, thick and big.

He looked at her with hooded eyes, kneeling down at the foot of the bed, pulling her close to its edge. He removed the tiny scrap of lace covering her private area with just his mouth, making her gasp when his breath touched her inner thighs.

And she found herself wetting her dry lips with her tongue while she watched him. Without warning, Elijah parted her legs wide open and stared at her hole, making her blush crazily.

She was wet.

It was her first time. And having someone watching her closely like that, was beyond all the embarrassment she had experienced before.

"Fuck!" he cursed in between her legs. She closed her eyes when the tip of his tongue slid along her entrance.

Meredith groaned with pleasure when she felt his finger slide inside her. She was so wet that it slid in easily. He felt so damn good.

But she wanted more.

As if reading her mind, Elijah started rubbing his tongue against her clit, and she shuddered in ecstasy. The feeling he was giving her was new, and it was driving her insane. When he inserted another finger, she heard herself squeaking in pleasure as he continued licking her pussy.

She was dripping, and more than ready for him to satisfy her needs. She thought she was losing her mind. How could she not? His touch was taking her higher and higher. She felt like she was floating on air.

Her fingers ran through his hair, pulling him closer.

"Please," she begged.

"Yes?"

"Just fucking do it," she spoke while panting heavily.

Her eyes widened when Elijah stroked his cock a few times before lining himself up in between her legs. She felt a bit scared. She'd heard the first time was painful, and she was worried he was too big for her.

"Please be gentle," she murmured, biting his bottom lip.

"I thought you wanted me to fuck you?" he said with a smirk.

"It's…" she whimpered in pleasure as his hands squeezed her breasts, " It's my first time," she said.

Meredith wished she hadn't said anything when Elijah froze. Without a word he climbed off the bed, moving to pick her dress up off the floor.

"Get dressed," he said.

"What?" She was confused. She wanted him, and she knew he wanted her. They'd finally been about to fuck. And now he was telling her to get dressed?

"Get dressed and go back to your room," he said patiently, although his tone was icy.

"Seriously?" she grumbled in disbelief, picking up her dress and underwear, feeling mortified more than ever.

She'd been more than ready to lose her virginity to him. And here he was, kicking her out. She felt insulted.

"Let's not talk about this. See yourself out," he said without looking at her.

With that, Elijah locked himself in the bathroom, leaving her speechless. She was mad.

Mad as hell.

She must have been out of her mind to think she'd lose her virginity with him.

No way!

18

---

fter checking in to their hotel in Texas, Eli immediately headed for a meeting with his speechwriters. But as much as he wanted to focus, his mind constantly wandered to thoughts of Meredith. Mostly of the moment they'd shared in his hotel room.

He'd never imagined she was still a virgin.

And he hadn't expected her to be willing to give it up to him.

Part of him was flattered. But a larger part, for some reason, was scared. Touching her would mean he'd have to take responsibility for whatever happened next. And he wasn't sure he was ready for something like that.

But damn! A woman in her twenties, still a virgin? Dude, that's rare, he thought, making him shake his head.

Meredith herself was rare. He must have been out of his mind for turning her down.

But if he'd had sex with her that night, it would have been his first time taking a woman's virginity. He'd never slept with a virgin before. He wondered what it would be like.

Just the idea of how incredibly tight she must be started to make his dick hard.

Fuck.

"Are you okay?" Lea asked, looking concerned. She was his head speechwriter.

"Yeah," he answered, wiping away cold beads of sweat from his forehead.

"You can leave everything to us, Elijah. Don't worry too much. Get some rest. You're looking a bit pale," Lea said, looking worried.

"Are you sure?" he asked.

"Yep! I'll call you if we need anything," she answered. He shot her a grateful smile.

Relieved, he headed back to his room, fully intending to get some sleep. Everything had been so hectic lately, and he'd been getting less sleep than normal.

But when he passed by Meredith's room, he was knocking on her door before he could reconsider what a terrible idea this was. He just wanted to see her face. When the door swung open moments later, he found himself stunned into silence.

Meredith was wearing a pink tank top and denim shorts. She wasn't wearing any makeup, and she looked like she'd just finished drying her hair. Even like this, he found her incredibly beautiful.

"Hi," he said stiffly, feeling awkward.

They hadn't talked since that night – he'd suspected she'd been avoiding him. He felt like a giant asshole for the way he'd treated her.

"Hi," she answered, lowering her head as her cheeks grew tomato red.

"Do you want to get something to eat?" he asked, thinking he could have done better than that.

She blinked.

"I don't think that's a good idea," she said hesitantly.

"Relax. Everyone will come with us. It'll be a group outing," he responded, disappointed by this turn of events. He hadn't really thought this through at all. And of course he wanted to be alone with her. But he didn't have a choice.

Being seen alone together would only prompt rumors.

"Fine," she said, then shut the door in his face. Well, at least she'd agreed, so that was something at least.

Heading down to the hotel lobby, Elijah called Sosie and instructed her to make the necessary arrangements. Sosie sounded irritated, but did as he asked.

It didn't take long before everyone was gathered in the lobby. Meredith was now wearing a pair of jeans and a white shirt, but she still looked stunning as usual. Sosie was running late, and texted him to say to go ahead without her, but to save her a seat next to him.

The only place able to accommodate their group on such short notice was more casual than he'd had in mind, serving mostly fried foods and cheap beer. No one seemed to mind though, and Eli was more than happy to sit next to Meredith.

When the food was served, he thought Meredith would politely decline. But to his surprise, she was one of the first to dig in.

"Sorry I'm late you guys," he heard Sosie say behind him. "I had some things to wrap up," she added, trying to pull up a chair between him and Meredith.

It didn't escape Eli's notice when Sosie grimaced after seeing the assortment of fried foods on the table. Like Meredith, Sosie came from an obscenely wealthy family. But she was acting like she'd rather drop dead than eat any of this food.

"I never thought you'd like this kind of food, Miss Fields," Sosie said in a loud voice, drawing everyone's attention to Meredith.

"Oh? How come?" Meredith asked cautiously.

"Because you were born with a silver spoon in your mouth," Sosie said, and everyone stopped to stare. "I just assumed you only ate foods prepared by your own personal chef."

Meredith blushed furiously. She looked flustered and humiliated. She'd been working hard to keep a low profile from the start. He knew she never mentioned her family or anything about her background if she could help it.

"Of course not," Meredith answered cheerfully, putting a smile on her face, but he could tell it was forced.

"Really?"

"How rich?"

"How come you never mentioned anything?"

"Tell us about it!"

Everyone flooded Meredith with questions. As expected, Sosie appeared to be the only one enjoying this. It looked like a deliberate attempt to put Meredith on edge.

"Come on everyone, let's talk about something else. Meredith's personal life is her own business," he said.

He didn't like the way Sosie was acting. And he especially didn't like it when he saw tears in Meredith's eyes.

Everyone resumed eating and soon things reverted back to the relaxed atmosphere they'd been enjoying before Sosie had joined them.

Eli was distracted when Sosie clapped her hands, gathering the attention of the crowd once more. She looked happy, but waited until the table was silent before she spoke.

"I've got good news!" she exclaimed.

He didn't know what she was about to say, but he had a feeling it wasn't anything truly important. But Sosie loved making a big deal out of everything.

"What is it?" Ava asked.

"Eli's leading the polls! Isn't it great?" she said, throwing her arms around him as everyone clapped.

Everyone stopped when Miriam made a "pffft" sound.

"What's wrong?" Meredith asked.

"Everybody knew that Mr. Scott was leading in the polls. He's got the highest approval ratings, you know. I thought it was something better," Miriam answered.

"Like what?" Sosie questioned.

"Like, you know… You two, finally getting together," said David from the far end of the table that made everybody oooh and aaaahh.

Especially flattered, Sosie tightened her arms around his neck, squirming closer to him as if there was really something going on between them. But Elijah's eyes were glued to Meredith, who didn't say a word, but lowered her head instead.

"Come on, guys. It's not like that," Sosie said. "Eli and I are just friends," she added before leaning in closer.

He wanted to pull away from her and tell everyone she was full of shit. But he didn't want her to lose face. And if he denied everything, he knew it would just lead to more gossip and rumors.

Looking at Sosie, he saw her glaring at Meredith. It was incredibly absurd and childish.

After a few minutes later, Meredith and everyone else called it a night, saying they were going back to the hotel to finish some work. But he knew the truth.

By now they were reporting to their editors about him supposedly dating his campaign manager.

When he was alone with Sosie, he said, "What the hell is all this about?"

Her eyes narrowed. He knew she was doing it on purpose.

"You know damn well what this is all about, Elijah. Despite me telling you to stay away from her, you've been flirting with Meredith Fields. And maybe even more than flirting," she said accusingly.

"I have not been flirting with her, okay?" he said.

She rolled her eyes. "I'm not an idiot, Elijah. But clearly you are. I'm firing her first thing in the morning," she said.

"You can't do that," Elijah murmured, his hands clenching into fists.

"Actually, as your campaign manager, I can. A big part of my job is making sure you keep the squeaky clean image that's going to get you elected. No more jailbait, no more temptation," she said in a mocking tone.

"No!" he said firmly, a little too loud, which startled Sosie into silence.

It took her a couple of moments to react. But her expression remained shocked and confused.

"I was right. You like her," Sosie concluded as tears welled in her eyes.

She was hurt.

But there was no point in trying to reason with her. He knew she'd never hear him out.

"Meredith will stay. Her father is too important. We can't fire her," he said, not even bothering to deny Sosie's accusation.

She eyed him angrily. She knew he was right. It was the very same thing she'd told him from the start.

It was impossible to fire Meredith Fields.

"I promise. I'll stay away," he said, raising his hands in the air, to end the conversation.

He hoped he could keep that promise.

But he seriously doubted it.

19

When they got to Arizona, only a few people decided to go horseback riding. Meredith hadn't been on a horse in years but she went along with Miriam, Ava, David and a few more people from the team – and Elijah.

After the humiliating encounters Sosie had been putting her through, she felt more than a little relieved when the woman stayed behind, saying she disliked horses.

As they rode uphill, she took a deep breath, enjoying the fresh air for the first time in a long time.

Meredith felt like she was back on vacation as she looked at the green fields. It was a refreshing view since all she had seen these past weeks were skyscrapers and endless highways.

When she got to a split path with several directions to choose from, Meredith selected the one that seemed to lead to the woods, nudging her horse. She didn't know Elijah followed her as the others went down other paths.

Closing her eyes, she relaxed, feeling the summer breeze touching her face. She felt so good she wished she could stay like that forever.

"So, you've been horseback riding before?" she heard Elijah's familiar voice ask from behind her. She maneuvered the ropes and nudged her horse with her feet to make it turn in his direction.

She looked around to see if anyone else was with them.

But there was no one else.

They were alone together – again.

"Just a few times," she answered with a shrug. "When I was in high school, my dad usually took me and my sister for lessons whenever he had the time."

"You must have been so happy," he said softly, the words barely escaping his mouth.

She frowned.

"Why do you say that?" she asked.

"Money's never been an issue for you. What it's like to lead such a life?" he asked, which made her chuckle a little.

She knew that's what they all thought. That just because she was born rich, she was happy. But that was far from reality.

All of her family's wealth couldn't buy them happiness.

It had been obvious to Meredith since she was a little girl that her parents weren't in love with each other. Their relationship was one of convenience and companionship. If they loved each other, it was only because they'd been together for more than two decades.

"I don't think there's a way to answer that question. All I know is that I'm thankful for the life I've been able to lead," she stated plainly, hoping she didn't sound like she was boasting.

They fell into a comfortable silence as they rode beside a stream, stopping occasionally to let their horses drink and graze. She thought she'd ask him about his personal life as well.

"What about you? It's not like you're hurting for money these days," she said.

Elijah smirked.

"I joined the military for a variety of reasons, one of the main ones being that they'd pay for college. After I got out, I worked as a military contractor. And then I became politically active, and the rest is history, or at least I'm hoping it'll be," he said with a grin. She sensed he was holding something back though.

"What was the main reason you joined the Navy?" she asked out of curiosity.

He fell silent, his eyes looking at the far horizon.

"I lost several of my friends during 9/11, and I couldn't just do nothing," he murmured.

She was speechless. She couldn't even imagine how hard it must have been for him. Her heart went out to him.

When Elijah noticed her silence, he prodded his horse, cantering off to the end of the stream where an old tree stood strong. He got off his horse to let it drink and she followed him, doing the same thing.

But being the clumsy girl that she was, she lost her balance as she tried to remove her feet from the saddle. She closed her eyes when she realized she was falling, uttering a silent prayer that she wouldn't get heavily injured.

They were almost halfway through the campaign, and she couldn't afford to back out at a time like this. As much as she hated to admit it, she was starting to enjoy the pressures of her job.

Meredith held her breath as she waited for her body to land on the hard ground. But she landed on something else. When she opened her eyes, she met Elijah's gaze, looking down at her with a concerned expression.

He'd caught her.

"Are you okay?" he asked worriedly.

She nodded in response, feeling like a thorn was stuck in her throat. Her eyes continued to look deep into his grey ones, where she found herself at peace. And the warmth coming from his embrace made her feel like she was at home.

She held her breath when his arms tightened around her waist, pulling her closer to his body.

When Elijah leaned in, she closed her eyes as their lips touched. It was a tender kiss – slow, soft and not at all demanding. They were taking their time, enjoying each other, as if they had all the time in the world.

Meredith felt lightheaded when he deepened the kiss, his tongue probing her mouth. And she obliged, letting their tongues dance together.

She moaned sexily, wanting far more than just a kiss.

But Elijah pulled away. He looked dazed as he helped her get back on her feet.

"I can't do this," he mumbled helplessly.

"I know," she said and nodded. She understood his point, and she knew all too well it would be impossible.

Feeling ashamed of herself, she got back on her horse and made sure everything was fine. She nudged the stallion to turn about when Elijah spoke.

"I'm so sorry, Meredith. If it wasn't for the election… Maybe…" he muttered softly.

Without a word, she maneuvered her horse and let it run back to the path they took earlier.

Maybe… Just maybe…

20

The campaign bus was in the middle of the road. They were on the second leg of the campaign, and Eli was more distracted than ever. Lately it seemed like he was constantly angry or upset. And it wasn't a good thing.

Sosie had been nagging at him endlessly, and it was making him angrier each time she laid into him.

He was going mad.

After making a few calls to donors, he decided to call Henry. He wasn't sure if asking his friend for advice would be a good thing or not. But at least he'd be able to vent a little.

He was distracted and bothered because of her.

It was all because of her.He dialed Henry's number, and it only took a few seconds before he answered.

"Hey, Eli. What's up?" Henry greeted him, holding a slice of pizza in his left hand.

He sighed.

"I'm in trouble," he grunted.

"What? Why?"

"There's this woman–"

"Whoa! Woman! That's big trouble, man," Henry cut him off, then chuckled before biting his pizza.

"It is," he agreed, rolling his eyes.

"So is she hot?" Henry asked.

"That's not the point – but of course she is. So fucking hot, I can't get her off my damned mind," he murmured as pictures of Meredith flashed in his mind. And he groaned when the memory of them making out replayed in his brain.

Henry laughed heartily, annoying the hell out of him.

"You're talking about the blonde from the party, right? Go on, tell me," Henry urged him after taking gulping down some water.

Eli paused, not knowing where to start his story.

"Okay, we've talked and she was so different. The girls I've dated in the past were nothing like her. She was someone I never expected to meet. She was just... beautiful. Inside and out," he stated. He didn't even know if it made any sense. All he knew was that he was having a hard time to explain how and why he'd ended up like this.

"How far have you gone with her?" Henry asked, his tone serious. But his eyebrows wiggled mischievously.

"To bed," he answered shortly.

"Oh, that's fast. Why are you even telling me this? You already slept with her," Henry grunted, rolling his eyes.

"I haven't. I mean, yes, we made out. But I stopped. Nothing happened. We did not have sex," he spoke, emphasizing each word as it left his mouth.

"What?!"

"She's a fucking virgin! How could I?" he retorted while gritting his teeth.

"And she was willing to give it to you?" Henry asked with amusement.

"Look, this isn't funny."

"I thought you were trying to stay single?" he questioned with a smirk on his face.

"I was! And I still am," he answered in a low voice. "I have a lot of stuff going on. But it's getting harder to focus with her around."

Henry laughed again like he was watching a comedy.

"What's so funny, you idiot?" he asked angrily.

"Man, you're acting like a man who has found love, but is too stupid to know what to do with it."

Elijah froze. What? Him? In love?

He shook his head. Yes, he was attracted to Meredith but falling in love with her was something else entirely. He wasn't even sure what falling in love meant. And it was just…

Impossible…

"I barely know her," he found himself mumbling. Was he trying to convince himself? Or Henry?"I'm just calling it like the way I see it," the man answered with a grin plastered on his face. He looked like he was about to say something more.

But Elijah was too flustered by his friend's offhand comment to continue the conversation. Maybe he just needed to organize his thoughts. And maybe...

Just maybe…

"I'll see you the next time I'm home," he said, pressing the end call button.

Maybe he really had fallen in love with Meredith Fields.

21

During yet another press briefing, Meredith was finding it difficult, if not impossible to concentrate. Seeing her name on bylines had made this all worth it.

It was an accomplishment she could be proud of, something she'd earned on her own merits. She was ecstatic.

She felt terrific!

Elijah was fielding questions now from the crowd. Periodically she would look up from her articles to find him looking directly at her.

She was flattered. But he was obviously distracted by her presence. For the first time since she'd met him, he was struggling to answer questions at times. What had happened to his focus?

I hope he's doing fine, she thought as she went back to her room.

After taking a quick shower, she changed into a tank top and shorts, feeling like it would make her feel more comfortable. She did her skincare routine, then threw herself on the bed when it was finished.

Finally! Early bedtime as a reward for all those sleepless and tiring days, she thought gleefully as she turned off the lights.

She was still smiling as she counted the number of published articles with her name on them. It was so dreamy, she thought she was losing her mind. Who would have thought she'd be able to achieve such a feat?

But at the back of her mind, she thought something was lacking. She was happy, but she didn't feel complete. It was as if something was left out of the picture. And she couldn't pinpoint what that something was, exactly.

Shrugging off such silly thoughts, she closed her eyes and decided to finally try and get some sleep.Her mind wandered, thinking of the intense sensations Elijah's touch had provided her. The memory of her lying underneath him as he was about to enter her looped in her mind on repeat.

She bit her bottom lip.

How could she forget how good it made her feel whenever he kissed her passionately? His touch made her defenseless. She knew it was crazy, but just the mere brushing of their skin took her breath away. His kisses were the sweetest.

Elijah Scott's touch was magic.

And she thought she wouldn't mind getting bewitched by him.

Only him.

She swallowed hard when she remembered how big and thick he was. She knew she was having more and more perverted thoughts these days. But when it came to Elijah, she couldn't help it. How could she? Especially when she could definitely see herself losing her virginity to him.

Knowing Elijah was like an introduction to a new flavor of ice cream to her.

With him, she was willing to be submissive; she was perverted; she was wild. And it was her first time thinking about how great it would have been to be fucked like that.

Yes, she wanted him to fuck her brains out.

She wanted her first time to be memorable.

She wanted him to be her first.

God, she fucking wanted him!

Meredith gritted her teeth, cursing under her breath for thinking about sex when she should have been fast asleep.

She was horny.

As she debated whether to touch herself or not, a knock on her door caught her attention, making her roll her eyes in annoyance. Who in the world would want something from her?

Getting up from her bed, she grabbed a robe and put it on, tying a loose knot at the waist.

"Hi," Elijah greeted when she swung the door open. Her face was mere inches from his chest. And she swallowed hard when she smelled his familiar, comforting scent. He smelled so damn good.

Meredith raised her head to meet his gaze.

He looked confused and hesitant.

But she wasn't.

She looked to either side of the hallway to see if anyone was there. When she was certain no one else was around, she pulled Elijah inside her room – fearless and excited.

Tonight is going to be my first time, she thought when she slammed the door shut.

Elijah looked flustered at first, but his expression immediately changed. His eyes turned dark with intense thirst as he stared at her from head to toe.

Meredith blinked, realizing the robe's knot had come undone, revealing her hard nipples underneath her thin tank top.

Her mind wasn't functioning very well as her heart throbbed hard against her chest. She was nervous. But she thought it would be a whole lot better if he'd just throw his arms around her and kiss her already.

As if reading her mind, Elijah pinned her against the wall, pushing her hands above her head, kissing her savagely. It was a kiss full of want and longing, and it took her breath away. It was intense and exciting.

She responded and matched his pace as his tongue probed her mouth. She loved it whenever he did that. The kiss went deeper.Elijah pulled away, giving them both a chance to catch their breath.

"What are you doing?" she asked.

With his hands running down her spine, he looked her straight in the eyes with a mixture of confusion, fondness and desire. He looked like someone who had been struggling inwardly.

What was bothering him so much?

”You,” he spoke, answering the question on her mind. “I can't think straight because of you. I can't fucking get you out of my mind, Meredith. Why are you doing this to me?” he grumbled under his breath. It was evident on his face that he was being sincere.

She stiffened, not knowing how to respond.

Did she really have that kind of effect on him?

Pulling her close, Meredith felt his breath against her neck. His throat pulsed as her breasts touched his chest, igniting the spark between them into fire. She looked at his eyes and felt like she was about to spontaneously combust.

“You shouldn't have let me come in here,” Elijah spoke huskily, each word heavy.

She gasped when his hands traveled to her breasts, cupping them in his hands. His mouth landed on hers, devouring her with such intense hunger. And she obliged, responding to his kisses with more need and want.

He was a predator. And she was his willing prey. She loved the way he touched her.

Elijah's mouth curled into a smile against her lips, delighted with her response.

“I'm taking everything that belongs to me,” he spoke, freeing her breasts from her top, kneading them before licking and sucking her nipples.

She whimpered in pleasure as he teased her.

He was driving her mad. And she wanted to settle things between them once and for all.

"Take me," she murmured in between heavy breaths. "I'm yours."

22

*R*unning his hand along her bare leg, Elijah couldn't help but grunt at the feel of her satin skin against his cool palm. He pulled her shorts down as his fingers slowly crept between her thighs.

He was finally ready to take her – and her virginity.

Meredith was the only woman who had given him the most agonizing rock-hard erection in his entire existence. And he swore nothing and no one could stop him now. This time, he would definitely take what was rightfully his.

She belonged to him.

She was his.

He grinned as he stroked her tense thigh, willing her to relax under his touch.

Since the night at the party, Meredith had been stuck in his head whether he liked it or not. She was sexy. She was naughty. And he knew she wanted great sex for her first time.

Eli had always been a predator and whenever he wanted a woman, he claimed her. If not for the election, he would have already had her.

When he'd learned she was still a virgin, he'd really messed things up between them. He'd been scared – and confused of the feelings he had for her. He didn't know what to do with her. Part of him had felt like maybe she was too precious for him to touch.

Hell, he'd never feared touching a woman before. But Meredith was different…

Then he became obsessed with being her first.

And tonight, he was willing to risk everything to have her.

He'd help her find her limits. He'd teach her to trust.

To trust him.

Eli lifted her thick blonde hair and pressed his lips against her skin, flicking his tongue along her flesh. He smiled when he felt her nails dig into his back. And he loved the traces of salty sweat, and the hint of her rose-scented soap.

Delicious, he thought.

"Mmmm…" she moaned sexily, making him smile. It sounded like an angel's voice in his ears. She was so fucking horny for him.

Meredith started rocking back and forth slowly and seductively. He wanted to take it slow – to take their time. But she was making it harder for him – and his cock.

He cursed under his breath.

When he slid his hand around her upper thigh and cradled her ass, his brows lifted in surprise when his fingers encountered nothing but her soft skin. His cock jerked up against the zipper of his jeans. He'd been so focused on her breasts, he hadn't noticed she wasn't wearing underwear, until now.

"You're not wearing underwear," he commented huskily.

A very specific thought occurred to him.

"What were you doing before I came?" he asked with a grin, thinking about how naughty she could be. When her face flushed, he assumed he'd been right.

"I– I… I was just…" she trailed off as she looked away, directing her attention to the floor.

"You were what?" he teased, finally touching her wet folds.

He was right.

She was horny.

And he was willing to bet she'd been touching herself before he'd arrived .

"I–"

"It's okay, babe. No need to explain," he said laughing, licking his fingers that had touched her pussy, tasting her juices – tasting her.

Placing his hand back on her ass, she parted her legs slightly. Eli took it as an invitation. He trailed his fingers back up. He stroked his fingers along her hot, wet cunt.

He grinned when she gasped.

He then bent over and nibbled on her neck again. And she whimpered while tilting her head so that her hair spilled over him.

He closed his eyes, savoring what was hearing. He loved hearing her moans.

"You're so wet," he whispered, pressing two fingers against her clit.

Meredith moaned, biting her lower lip. And he continued circling his fingers over her in a lazy way that made her eyes grow wider.

Eli swore that he'd take things slowly to make sure Meredith would never forget about this night. He wanted her to have the best orgasm of her life. Pleasuring her was his number one priority.

"That feels so good," she spoke in between sighs, bracing herself as her head arched back in pleasure.

Elijah felt his cock throb inside his jeans as he watched her breasts heave with her every movement.

"Touch me," he invited, keeping his voice low and seductive.

Like an obedient child, Meredith ran her hand up his leg. She pressed her open palm against the bulge in his pants.

He moaned.

They'd almost had sex in his room before. But Eli swore that this time was on another level. It was like they were both completely certain of what they wanted – to satisfy each other's needs.

Eli's hips bucked when her hands slid along the zipper of his pants, following the line of his throbbing cock.

His head felt light as his cock grew bigger and harder in her hand.

"God, you're so big," she said, her eyes widening as her hand coasted over his rigid shaft.

He groaned at her touch.He parted the lips of her pussy with his fingers. He dipped into her wet hole, curling his fingers against the sensitive bundle of nerves along her front wall for a split second before pulling out. He inhaled her scent, loving the way she smelled.

Her blue eyes glazed over with desire as she continued squeezing his cock through his jeans.

With a smirk on his face, he plunged his finger into her pussy. Her creamy walls clamped around his finger, and his thumb rubbed the tip of her clit.

"Oh, god!" she moaned against his ears.

He kissed her soft and slightly parted mouth. He shifted his hand to fill her tight pussy with two fingers, stroking her ass while teasing her clit.

"Fuck! Fuck!"

His cock throbbed as she sank her teeth into his shoulder.

Gritting his teeth, he scooped her small figure into his arms and led them to her empty bed. He couldn't draw this out any longer. He thought he'd be able to take things slow, but that was proving impossible.

He wanted her so fucking bad.

And he was more than ready to fuck her.

Meredith looked him in the eyes with such intense need.

After stripping her down, he took a moment to admire her beautiful body, which only made him grow harder.

Without breaking eye contact, he stood in front of her, taking off his clothes piece by piece. He wanted her to see him clearly. He wanted her to remember that he was the man who took her virginity. He wanted all of this seared indelibly into her soul.

He wanted her to remember him as the man who had given her the wildest sex of her life.

Fully undressed, they stared at each other. And when she smiled shyly, he pulled her closer, wrapping his arms around her waist. He planted a deep and ravenous kiss on her mouth.

Her hands traced down his spine then back up, exploring his lean and strong shoulders. And she shuddered when he sucked on her hardened nipples, gasping as he continued groping her breasts.

Slowly, he laid her against the sheets. Then, he parted her legs as his eyes continued to roam over her body. When she licked her lips with her tongue, he grumbled, leaving a trail of kisses on her temple, brows, eyes, nose, and cheeks. His mouth traveled to her neck then to her shoulders, leaving not a spot untouched.

He stopped at the crook of her neck and nibbled on her sensitive skin.

Meredith touched his chest, tracing the trail of the tiny hairs that led down his abdomen. She reached for his hardened cock but halted when he started biting her nipples softly.

She moaned in ecstatic pleasure, her voice echoing in the corners of her room.

Pleased with her response, he showered her belly with tiny kisses. His hands continued cupping, kneading and groping her breasts. He smirked while she arched her body and her legs wrapped around his waist.

"You're so beautiful, Meredith!" he exclaimed, stimulated by her sexy moans.

He spread her legs apart impatiently, then placed his head between her legs.

"Oooohhhh! God!" she moaned as he took a quick taste of her pussy.

"I know you're going to like this," he mumbled against her clit, not wasting a single drop of her juices.

Eli felt her fingers running through his hair, tugging at his head. And to his surprise, Meredith pulled him closer to her opening, letting his tongue enter her deeper.

Inserting two fingers inside her, she made a squeaking sound. He pumped in and out of her just enough to get her ready for him. He made sure that he didn't go too deep.

Her virginity was for his cock.

"Oh… Ohhh… Shit!" she cursed as she shuddered when her walls contracted around his fingers as his tongue continued probing her clit.

Meredith buried her nails in his back as she gritted her teeth. But he stopped fingering her when she arched her back. She was about to cum again.

But he wasn't going to let her.

This time, they'd cum together.

Pinning her down, he seared her mouth, his tongue sweeping inside her slightly parted lips. His cock ached to be inside her.

Eli positioned himself in between Meredith's legs, lining his cock up at the entrance to her needy pussy. He looked at her widened eyes.

"I'll be gentle, I promise," he murmured under his breath, reassuring her.

She nodded her head in response.

Slowly, he inserted the head of his shaft and she gasped in pain. Tears pooled at the corners of her eyes as her nails dug in his back. She was in pain, and it broke his heart seeing her that way.

"Just tell me to stop if you want me to stop," he said softly.

"No, just go on. I can handle it," she answered firmly.

With that, he filled her with his length in one thrust, searing her mouth with a kiss so that he could keep her mind busy.

He had taken her virginity.

He was her first.

Eli pulled away from the kiss to let them catch their breath, and he watched Meredith grit her teeth. She was still in pain.

"Are you okay?" he asked worriedly, pushing away the strands of hair from her sweaty face. "Pain is only temporary, babe. Pleasure will take over."

As much as he wanted to feel her tight walls around him again, he wanted to make sure she was okay.

"You can move," she uttered breathily with a faint smile on her lips.

With that, Eli started sliding in and out of her. He wrapped his arms around her to make her feel more secure. His pace was slow at first, and when Meredith's whimpers were replaced with moans of pleasure, he increased his speed.

"Ohh… Yeah…" she wailed.

"You like that?" he asked.

"That feels so fucking good, Elijah!" she screamed, arching her back.

Feeling motivated, he pounded deeper and harder. He rocked his body, rotating his hips, breathing heavily and grunted at how good she was making him feel. And he could tell that she, too, was enjoying the way he fucked her.

"Oh, fuck me Elijah!" she begged.

Eli moved in and out of her in demanding strokes as he could feel his orgasm nearing. Meredith's moans and whimpers were driving him insane. It was like a little pill that brought him to heaven.

He devoured her mouth once more when he felt her walls quiver around him.

She was cumming.

Meredith's legs locked around his waist for support as her back left the sheets, arching her body to meet the strokes of his cock inside her.

"Virgin no more," he muttered with a smirk. "And now, you're mine."

"I'm yours, Elijah," she responded, pulling his head down for a kiss as he slammed into her with one last thrust, releasing his load while she came violently.

They shared one more passionate kiss before he collapsed on top of her as they struggled to get their breath back. Looking at her eyes, he pushed the strands of her blonde hair behind her ears and kissed her temple.

He was happy.

No, happy was an understatement.

He felt complete – and fulfilled.

Eli nibbled on Meredith's shoulder as they shared the comfort of silence for a few minutes.

"That was hot," she murmured, stroking his spine, which made his cock twitch.

"It was," he agreed, nibbling her earlobe once more.

"And you're hard again."

She giggled.

"Yeah, you have to take responsibility."

"It's not my fault if you have a perverted mind," she commented.

"I'm not alone here," he retorted with a smirk. "Who was touching herself?"

She blushed.

"I wasn't."

"You were going to. If I hadn't knocked," he pointed out.When she pouted, he knew he was right.

"Oh, shut up!" she grunted, wrapping her fingers around his cock without warning.

Elijah cursed as he groaned in pleasure with his eyes closed. He was all the more surprised when he saw her licking the tip of his cock when he opened his eyes.

"That's cheating," he grunted, gritting his teeth. He leaned back as his head felt overwhelmed with the sensations coming from her lips.

Damn! His dreams were finally turning into reality, and it was a million times better!

"I'm taking what's mine," she responded, her tongue traveling along the length of his shaft.

Eli hadn't been expecting that. But he wanted to just enjoy the moment. He was in her room, and he was hers for the taking. He'd let her do anything she wanted with him.

Nobody had to know about what happened tonight.

Tonight, they were no longer strangers to each other.

Tonight, she was his.

And he was hers.

23

*S*taring blankly at the ceiling, Meredith was sleeping soundly in Eli's arms. She looked so peaceful like this – and tired after all the wild sex they'd had. He didn't think he'd ever been so content after fucking a woman in his entire life, until now.

He'd been surprised at how insatiable she'd been.

It was her first time, after all.

But she'd been more active and daring during rounds two and three. They'd came together three times in just under five hours.

He sighed, wondering what would happen next. The election prevented him from dating her openly, and his hands were tied.

Would she be able to settle for being friends with benefits for now?

He didn't have a chance, did he?

Is this what you want? he asked himself, tilting his head to look at Meredith's beautiful face.

But Eli knew more than anyone that he didn't want her to just be a fling, or to only be friends with benefits. He wanted more than sex from her.

He wanted her, it was as simple as that.

He wanted her as a person.

As a woman.

His attention was caught by the loud ringing of his phone, making him jump off the bed, not wanting to disturb Meredith's sleep. Who was calling him at three in the morning?

Frowning, he picked up his phone to check the caller ID. He broke out into a cold sweat when he saw the name on the display.

It was Vincent Johnson, an old friend from his time in the military. They'd been friends since high school though, and enlisted together after 9/11.

They hadn't been in contact for a long time.

And based on Vincent's attitude, he wouldn't call if it wasn't important – or urgent.Eli locked himself in the bathroom and answered the call as quietly as he could. He knew it would be classified information, too.

"Vincent, what made you call?" he asked the moment he answered.

"Damn, Elijah! You should have picked up sooner," the man hissed over the line.

He grimaced.

"What's the matter?" he asked, feeling worried. Something told him this wasn't about good news. Vincent never gave him good news.

"Ryan, your brother –"

"What happened to my brother?" he cut him off.

"Nothing happened," Vincent answered. "Yet."

"What do you mean?"

"His SEAL unit is due to be deployed on a dangerous mission," his friend informed.

Feeling like a bucket of cold water had been poured over him, Eli froze. Had he heard him right?

"What mission?" he questioned.

"I'm sorry, bro. It's classified," Vince replied apologetically, followed by a heavy sigh.

He closed his eyes, trying to think. Classified meant the expected survival rate for the mission would be less than forty percent, and that was probably generous. His younger brother could not go on that mission.

He couldn't let that happen – not to his family.

"Can you do something about it?" he asked hopefully.

He knew Vincent would try his best to help. They'd been buddies for a long time. And Eli had saved his life on more than one occasion back when he was still active duty.

"I'll see what I can do," Vincent replied hesitantly. "But I'm only doing this because I owe my life to you."

"Give the mission to another team," Eli said after a moment of silence.

He knew it was a selfish thing to ask. But he couldn't afford to lose a family member. Everything he was doing now was for his family's sake.

Whatever happened, he would never let his family perish.

"I will," Vincent responded.

"Thanks, dude. Thank you."

"No problem. I'll call you again."

Turning, he opened the bathroom door, only to find Meredith pressed against it. She was shocked, and it was obvious she'd been eavesdropping. He was certain she'd heard everything.

Anger surged through him.

But it quickly vanished when he got a good look at her. She had nothing but the blanket wrapped around her body. She looked like a child who'd just gotten up from bed.

"Please keep this a secret," he mumbled while picking up his clothes.

Everything was getting more and more complicated.

Why in the world was this happening to him?She nodded her head, unable to speak a word. She was clearly shaken up by what she had heard. *Welcome to the dark side of politics,* he thought as he watched her wrap the blanket tighter around herself, reminding him for all the world of a shroud.

24

True to her word, Meredith kept quiet about the conversation she'd overheard. But the strike went south, and soon it was all over the news.

A SEAL and civilians had died in the attack.

And it sounded so bad.

She felt remiss as a journalist for not writing about this, especially when she had inside knowledge. But she'd made a promise. And she wasn't about to break his trust for an article.

She didn't have the courage or the desire to end whatever it was they had. She couldn't call it a relationship, she knew that. But it was more than just sex to her.

During a press conference, the strike came up almost immediately when they opened the floor to questions. She could tell Elijah was struggling to find the right words to say.

They asked if he would condone these kinds of strikes if elected president.

She tried her best not to cringe.

It was a tricky question.

He answered in the safest possible way, referring to his experience as a SEAL and stating that his actions would depend on the situation and the intel available to him.

When the conference was over, she went to grab a bite to eat with Ava and Miriam. She had work to do, and it would hopefully distract her for a few hours.

Ava and Miriam started chatting about the conference. Both of them had noticed how tense Elijah's body language had been when they'd questioned him about the SEALs. Meredith decided to stay out of the conversation. She opened her laptop and started composing an e-mail to Mitch.

It would be better if she kept silent.

She was afraid her tongue would give her away.

"What about you? What do you think?" Ava asked, nudging her.

"I… don't really know. I'm not very familiar with the military," she murmured softly, trying her best not to choke on her words. "I grew up in a civilian family, as you guys know," she said quietly.

Yep, she didn't know a thing about the military in general. But she knew something – particularly on the current issue.

"Oh come on. He must have told you something," Miriam said while rolling her eyes.

"What do you mean?" she asked with a frown.

"I mean, he seems to like you," Miriam answered while Ava snickered.

Meredith froze. Had they really been that obvious?

Bored with the lack of substance in her replies, Ava and Miriam went on with their business in silence – just like everybody else was doing. She was glad she was able to shrug off their questions.

She hated lying.

But she'd do it – for Elijah.

After lunch, Meredith and the rest of the group went back to the hotel and headed to their own rooms. She was not sure if she could rest since her mind was filled with questions. Why was she keeping his secret? What would happen to her? To him? What would happen to them? Would everything be over in just a night?

Would it be just a night to remember?

Like an answer from heaven, there was a knock on her door. She quickly opened it and saw Elijah standing in front of her. He looked stressed.

"Hi," she whispered, checking the hallways.

"Hi," he replied hoarsely.

Without a word, she pulled him inside her room. She then sighed after locking the doors. She had a lot to ask him. But she didn't know where to start.

"Did you eat?" she ask.

It was stupid.

"Yeah, a bit," he replied.

"So…"

"I'm keeping your promise, Meredith. Nobody has to know about what you heard the last time," he spoke in between heavy breaths.

And that was enough for her to understand that he was still hesitant to trust her words. She'd promised him, hadn't she?

"I promised, didn't I? So get your act together because everybody thinks that your answers regarding the issue are weak," she retorted, feeling a bit insulted.

"What did you say?" he asked, alarmed.

"Nothing. There was nothing I could comment. Because seriously, I don't have any idea what to say," she responded while gritting her teeth.

Elijah sighed in relief. And it made her more annoyed. Was that the only thing he wanted to talk with her? What about her? What about them?

"Thank you," he mumbled sincerely. "I'm just worried. I'm sorry for doubting you."

"It's okay," she responded, trying to keep her tone neutral.

She was trying her best not to burst out crying. She never should have expected anything from him.

Sex.

It was just sex.

What was she thinking? She was the one who'd surrendered to him. She didn't have the right to feel bitter about it. He'd just granted her wish.

"I trust you," he said before planting a kiss on her forehead. "Thank you," he added before turning on his heels, leaving her frozen in place.

With that very simple gesture, Meredith felt a whole lot better. Maybe she was just overthinking things. She thought she should be more considerate of his situation.

For now, she should be content with whatever they have.

25

For the last leg of the campaign they were joined by Ellie Scott, Elijah's little sister. He was happy for the company though. It had been ages since they'd had any quality time together.

They were at a huge county fair. He was pleased by the huge crowd that had come out to see him, all of them cheering and waving around miniature flags with his name on them. The sun was scorching hot, but he didn't feel bothered by it.

He was just so happy with the support the people were showing him. Just like at all the other events, he delivered his speech flawlessly.

When his speech ended, people screamed, cheered and whistled and it was more than enough to quench the thirst he was feeling. He'd been to a lot of events, but that was the first time he'd seen a crowd who looked extremely happy to see him.

His eyes landed on Ellie who was watching him proudly, her hair bouncing as she jumped on her feet. She, too, was holding a little flag with his name on it, showing her support for his candidacy.

He couldn't be happier.

He was with a family member, and…

Looking around, his eyes searched for Meredith who was wildly scribbling on her notepad. She was wearing a sun visor, and her hair was pulled into pigtails. There were beads of sweat on her face. But it didn't diminish the fact that she shone as bright as the sun that day.

Yes, he felt complete.

Because Meredith was there, too.

The fair was literally an amusement park. And he thought it would be a great chance to let everybody have a little bit of fun. Ellie especially looked like she was itching to get on all the free rides.

Eli instructed Sosie to tell the rest of the team to enjoy their time at the fair. He followed Ellie around as she stopped at every single booth like it was her first time at a county fair.

Shaking his head, he watched as Ellie repeatedly won the top prize at a booth set up to resemble a shooting range. The booth owner looked puzzled at first, then scowled when Ellie kept winning.

"Ellie, that's enough," he whispered to her, although he had to admit it was a little funny.

He was proud that his sister's skills hadn't gone rusty.

After leaving the military, Elijah brought Ellie on shooting ranges once or twice a month. He thought she needed to know how to use a gun just in case. His siblings were sharpshooters, thanks to him.

He was their mentor, after all.

Pouting, Ellie gave the toy gun back to its owner and gathered the pile of stuffed toys she had won. She gave up almost everything, handing the toys to children passing by, but kept the largest teddy bear for herself.

"Are you sure you're keeping that?" he asked, wincing. It was too big to carry around comfortably.

"Yep," she murmured, eyeing him.

"What?"

"You carry it," she stated, immediately turning on her heels, skipping to the next booth that caught her eye.

People looked at him as he walked around with the giant teddy bear, but their stares didn't bother him. Ellie forcing him to carry it bothered him. But he could never say no to his baby sister.

"Let's get on the Ferris wheel!" Ellie suggested, looking up at the ride.

"Seriously?"

"I'm getting cotton candy. You want some?' she asked instead.

"Nah, I'm fine. Go on," he answered while rolling his eyes as he waited for her to get the tickets and treats.

Ellie had just turned twenty six, and she was one of the main reasons why he'd gone into politics. He wanted to give his sister a better life.

It didn't take long before she was back in front of him. And she literally had to drag him to the Ferris wheel.

"Come on, Eli!" she pleaded, looking at him with puppy dog eyes.

He grimaced.

"You're not a kid anymore."

"I'm a kid at heart," she said, sticking her tongue out at him playfully.

"Whatever," he grumbled as they got on the ride.

He settled the teddy bear next him carefully.

As the Ferris wheel moved, they talked about her plans after graduating high school.

"What about you? What's up with you?" she asked, pinching off small pieces of cotton candy and delicately eating them.

He frowned, not sure he understood the question.

"I'm running for president," he said, stating the obvious.

Ellie rolled her eyes.

"That not what I meant. I mean what's up with you and the cute blonde," she asked.

Elijah almost cringed when Ellie looked at him with sparkling eyes, obviously interested in what he had to say. She wasn't usually the curious type. And this was the first time she'd ever asked him about his love life.

He made a face. He didn't want to talk about it, and especially not with his little sister.

"What do you mean? There's nothing between me and Meredith," he said, hoping she'd believe him and just drop it.

It was becoming increasingly harder to lie.

Really, you fucked her and took her virginity. Nothing between you two? Seriously? asked a voice in his mind sarcastically.

Eli knew that deep down, he wanted more than just sex with Meredith. In fact, it was getting tougher to maintain this facade each day that passed. He wished he could be with her more often.

"Meredith... Even her name is cute," Ellie commented while looking out over the fair. "You know I just want for you to be happy, right?" she said.

Elijah blinked at the seriousness and sincerity in his sister's voice. For a moment there, he thought she was really acting like an adult. But it all vanished when he flashed her a mischievous grin.

Who was he kidding? Elli would always be a kid – a playful one.

"I'll talk to her when we get down," she said, then focused her attention on her dwindling cotton candy.

Elijah didn't bother trying to talk her out of it. His little sister was the most stubborn person he'd ever met. What Ellie wanted, Ellie would get.

When the Ferris wheel stopped, Ellie hopped off it excitedly, skipping toward the booth where she'd last spotted

Meredith. He shook his head when his sister hooked arms with Meredith, surprising the latter.

He wanted to get a better look at the two, but he started sneezing.

Damn this stuffed animal, he cursed, walking away to find their rental car.

Elijah was sweaty and tired when he got to the car, throwing Ellie's teddy bear into the rear. He never should have taken it with them.

He frowned when his phone started ringing even before he could rest his eyes.

It was Sosie.

"Where are you?" she questioned.

"I'm in the car."

"Ellie has been going around with Meredith. You better take care of this before rumors start circulating. Either get your ass back out here or call your sister," she said hissing.

Up until now, Sosie had been civil with him. After the incident of her drunkenly throwing herself at him, she'd started to grow more irritable. He thought she was probably feeling embarrassed after getting rejected.

He couldn't blame her.

He was partly at fault.

"Sosie, they're just having fun. What's wrong with that?"

"It's wrong because it's Meredith," she answered angrily, ending the phone call.

Feeling lethargic more than ever, Elijah dialed Ellie's phone number and told her to get back to the car or else he'd cut the head off of her teddy bear. It was a childishly absurd thing to say.

But with his sister, it was more than enough to make her come running in fear.

Shaking his head, he chuckled when she quickly ended the call. He caught the smiling expression of his driver before closing his eyes. His head was pounding, and it was killing him. Plus, the itchy feeling in his nose was driving him crazy.

Trying to calm himself, he took a few deep breaths until the itch in his nose went away. But his peace of mind did not even last five minutes when Ellie got in the car, slamming the door shut from her side.

She looked at him, glaring. She was mad.

"You mean, arrogant, bad human be–"

"Oh shut up, it's in the back," he grumbled, leaning back against the seat.

"Oh, oh," Ellie murmured, quickly checking her teddy bear.

"Don't get it near me. Its fur is making my nose itchy," he warned.

Ellie watched him for a while. She then raised her hands in the air, accepting defeat.

"Fine."

The first ten minutes of the trip back to the hotel was quiet, and he was more than pleased to have at least a few moments of peace. He assumed that Ellie was tired from going around the crowded fair since she wasn't usually quiet. But when he looked at her, she was gazing out the window, staring at nothing in particular.

Ellie sighed heavily.

She was deep in thought.

"You should date her," she blurted out suddenly.

Elijah blinked in surprise. Had he heard her right?

"What?"

"I said, you should date Meredith. I know you like her. You couldn't take your eyes off her half the time we were at the fair. And I know she likes you, too. She's a nice person, and I like her."

He shook his head and scoffed.

"Stop talking nonsense, Ellie. Nothing can ever happen between us," he grumbled.

"Why?"

"You know perfectly well why."

"Why? Because you're running for president? There's no rules about this kind of thing, you know," she said.

"Not officially, no, but think about how it would look to the public. If I started dating a reporter who was working for my campaign, I'd be crucified... and so would she. It wouldn't be fair to her, Ellie."

His sister fell silent for a few moments.

"But you do like her, don't you?" It was more of a statement than a question.

He couldn't admit it to his sister, but he couldn't quite bring himself to say no either. Maybe he really did like her.

Or maybe Henry was right.

Maybe he was already in love with Meredith.

"I wouldn't want to be in your shoes," Ellie said and patted him on the shoulder. "Your life seems tough."

Furrowing his brow, he looked at her with questioning eyes. There was something in her expression that was making him want her to say more.

Ellie shrugged.

"You know, it's hard to look away from someone like Meredith. She's hot," Ellie stated dreamily before directing her attention back to the dark streets.

Doing the same, Elijah couldn't help but think his sibling was right. He was leading a tough life.

And Meredith was hot.

Fucking hot.

26

After planting a deep and passionate kiss on Elijah's lips, Meredith got out of bed – his bed. She looked at the messy sheets, unable to suppress her smile. They'd just had wild sex.

She loved having sex – with him. She felt practically addicted to fucking him.

"I wish you could stay longer," he whispered, nibbling on her shoulder as she picked up her clothes. She grimaced when she found her thong hanging on the lampshade.

She held her breath.

She felt the same.

She wanted to be with him the whole night and wake with him the next morning. She thought it would feel so damn good to be in his arms.

"Me too," she answered, blushing. She was embarrassed at the confession, but she thought it wouldn't be so bad to be more vocal about her feelings. They'd seen each other naked, what more was there to hide?

When Elijah nibbled her earlobe, she moaned as the sensations started overwhelming her. It was almost three in the morning and she needed to get out of there while everybody else was still asleep.

She knew she couldn't be seen.

"Elijah," she whimpered in protest as she started melting in his arms again. "Please, I have to go. I'm afraid people will see me if I leave a little late."

"I'm sorry," she murmured apologetically.

"No, Meredith. I'm sorry. All of this sneaking around is because of me," he said before walking toward the bathroom door. "I'll just take a shower. I don't want to see you leave. Be careful when you go out."

She nodded in response and continued getting dressed.

Checking her reflection in the mirror, she made sure she didn't look too disheveled. Because no matter what happened, she wouldn't let her appearance give her away.

She couldn't afford to be found out.

When she finally thought she looked respectable, she headed out. She was careful to look at her surroundings first before darting out of Elijah's room. She moved rapidly at first, but slowed her pace when she thought she was far enough away. Walking too fast would surely look suspicious.

"Meredith?" said a familiar voice, making her close her eyes and hold her breath. What was she doing up at this hour?

Turning on her heels, she saw Ava. She didn't bother asking her why she was still up. Her gym clothes were explanation enough.

"Ava!" she said, feigning surprise.

"What are you doing up? It's late," Ava asked, eyeing her from head to toe.

Her heart raced, but she controlled her breathing. She didn't need to feel nervous. She knew she looked normal.

"I went for a walk," she lied with a smile.

"At this hour?" Ava's eyes narrowed.

"Yeah," she answered with a nod, leading the way toward their bedrooms. They were in the same wing of the hotel.

"Is something bothering you?" Ava looked worried.

Meredith shrugged, feeling guilty for lying to her friend. But she didn't have a choice. She had to do it to protect Elijah's image.

"Just family stuff," she lied again.

"Oh, I wish I could be of more help."

"It's okay," she murmured, stopping in front of her door. "You should rest, too. It's getting late."

"Nah, I don't think I can sleep. I'll just read some good stuff. You rest," Ava said, waving goodbye.

"Okay, good night," Meredith answered.

"Good morning," Ava replied with a smile.

The moment she got inside her room, she released a loud and heavy sigh. She was so freaking nervous. But at the back of her mind, she regretted lying. She was never a good liar. She wished she could stop telling lies.

After getting a quick shower, she got in her pajamas and then lay on her bed while staring at the ceiling, waiting for sleep to claim her. But an hour passed, and she was still wide awake. Her mind was filled with questions and what ifs.

She groaned in frustration when her phone started ringing, making her frown. But her expression quickly changed when she saw Lily's name on the screen.

"What's up?" she greeted Lily.

"Oh my god! I've started to think you've forgotten about me! How come you never called me?" Lily squeaked, then pouted.

"I'm sorry. I've been so busy lately," she replied with a heavy sigh. "How's Bali?" she asked, feeling a momentary pang of regret for the summer she could have had if she'd gone traveling with Lily instead.

"It's so boring here. I'm heading to Ibiza in three days. I hear the party scene is better there anyway," Lily said, rolling her eyes.

"Oh, I see," Meredith responded, not the least bit excited about it.

What happened to you? You should be more ecstatic that there's another place where you can party 'till you drop!

"What's up with you?" Lily asked, narrowing her eyes.

Meredith tried to play dumb. "What?"

"You're not acting like your usual self, Mer. Come on, you can tell me anything."

"There's nothing to tell, really."

Lily pursed her lips. It was obvious from her expression that Meredith had failed to convince her of this.

"This is about Elijah Scott, right? Go on, spill the beans."

Meredith froze. It wasn't that she didn't want to tell Lily about everything. It was just that she wasn't sure where to start.

She took a deep breath.

"Something is going on between us," she said slowly, feeling a lump growing in her throat. "And… Actually, I just snuck out of his room."

Lily gasped, genuinely shocked. Meredith instantly regretted telling her, at least like this. She'd wanted to talk about this in person.

"Really?" Lily asked with gleaming eyes.

"Really," she repeated in affirmation.

"You slut! I can't believe you finally gave up your V-card!"

Meredith blushed. She was still embarrassed.

"Y-Yeah, I did."

"And?" Lily urged, wanting to get a few more juicy details.

"It was worth the wait, Lily," she answered honestly.

In fact, she thought it had been a whole lot better than what she had expected. It was not just a night to remember. It was – and would always be – a cherished moment.

Her first time had been a blast!

"You think you guys could be an item? Am I going to see you in the paper soon?" Lily asked excitedly. She was acting like a giddy teenager, anticipating the next episode of her favorite romantic sitcom.

Meredith swallowed hard.

"I… We haven't really talked about that. I don't know," she spoke in almost a whisper.

Lily gasped.

"Wait, so you two are doing it in secret?" the woman asked with an eyebrow raised.

"You make it sound so tawdry, Lily," she answered defensively.

"I'm just concerned for you, that's all. You waited all this time because you wanted it to be special and perfect, but now what? I don't like the idea of you being some politician's dirty little secret, Mer."

Meredith was taken aback. She hadn't expected Lily to be so blunt.

Was she going about this the wrong way?

Shrugging off the idea, Meredith shook her head. "It's not exactly like that."

"Well, what is it then?" Lily challenged.

"It's still so new. I don't want anything to disturb it," she muttered while pulling a face. She hated it when her best friend had a point.

Lily rolled her eyes like she'd just heard the stupidest joke of the year. She was openly showing her dislike of the situation.

"Whatever you say," the woman spoke dryly.

Meredith sighed.

"Listen… you never told me about that party on the yacht. How was it?" she asked, trying to change the subject.

As much as Meredith wanted to catch up with her best friend a little longer, she couldn't stop thinking about Lily's words. She knew Lily only wanted the best for her. And she knew the woman was right.

Sooner or later, she and Eli would have to put a label on whatever they were doing. And she didn't have the slightest idea how that would even happen.

But the real question was, would they even reach that part?

Dirty little secret.

Lily's words echoed in her mind until they said goodbye. She couldn't deny she was bothered by them. But she hoped things would get better soon.

27

After a successful campaign rally in Michigan, Eli attended yet another donor event. Sosie had been nagging him about optics, and he'd agreed to shake hands with everyone he met and kiss every baby he saw. The reporters followed him around as usual – snapping photos, taking notes, and asking questions.

He hadn't expected to enjoy the event. He'd never been fond of children. But today was different. He felt good around them for some unknown reason. He started to seriously entertain the idea of having kids of his own someday. He wondered if they'd have his eyes, or Meredith's...

What was he thinking? Lately he'd been thinking about things like settling down. This wasn't at all like him.

As he talked with a few people, his gaze traveled to Meredith again and again, unable to get enough of her. She looked so beautiful in her white floral skirt and black top. She looked like a runway model instead of a reporter.

He watched her laughing with colleagues as they sat in one corner to get some rest. And before he could even look away, she looked at him then smiled, sucking the end of her pen.

He blinked – stunned by the naughty gesture, making him forget what he was saying. A sudden rush of heat disturbed his thoughts, and she grinned when he looked at her again.

Damn. The woman really knew how to get under his skin.

Before sunset, the affair was wrapped up and they headed back to the hotel. Elijah desperately searched for Meredith's figure and when he found her, he pulled her into his limo, quickly rolling up the partition so the driver couldn't see them.

Without saying a word, he seared her mouth with a passionate kiss, pinning her down against the leather seat. Despite her shock, Meredith responded to his kisses with the same intensity. It was as if they hadn't spent the night together.

They just couldn't get enough of each other.

His hands traveled down her legs, caressing her soft skin. She squirmed underneath his touch, catching her breath as he pulled away, breaking their kiss. He cupped her breasts, her nipples hardening immediately as he brushed his thumbs over her peaks.

Meredith whimpered while watching him, her blue eyes full of desire.

She pulled off her top and quickly unhooked her bra. She moaned as his wet and warm mouth closed over one nipple, and he rolled the other between his thumb and forefinger.

He closed his eyes as he focused on sucking at her gorgeous tits, enjoying her delicate feminine taste. She tasted wonderful with the mixture of sweat and the traces of rose-scented soap on her skin.

She writhed under him as she released a muffled moan. He inhaled sharply, sliding his hands down to her ass. Her cheeks were bare, and he loved the way she felt in his hands.

"You're so wet," he whispered in her ear.

Meredith batted her lashes and arched her back in response, an invitation for him to do something about it.

Licking his fingers, he probed her slick and swollen flesh, fingering her clit. He knew his strokes were just about right when her grip on his shoulders tightened.

"Ooooh," she moaned huskily, trying her best to keep her voice subdued, which he found very sexy. Her legs wrapped around him, and he could tell that she was right on the edge when her jaw tensed.

So, he stopped.

"I have to see," he said.

Elijah went down on his knees, spreading her thighs wide. He opened her eagerly, wanting to see the glorious view of her wet folds. Just looking at Meredith's tight hole made him thirsty, and his cock jerked up against the zipper of his pants.

But he had a different motive.

He gave her pussy a languid lick, slowly teasing her, until she couldn't take it anymore and grabbed his head, grinding his face into her crotch.

He couldn't help but smile against her swollen clit. Meredith had gotten more and more naughty each time they'd had sex. Each time was more exciting than the last.

Sucking her clit, he inserted a finger inside her, earning himself a rewarding moan and gasps from her. He continued pleasuring her clit as he pumped his finger in and out of her tight walls.

Elijah felt his cock growing harder and bigger with each push inside her. She was so fucking tight, and his cock twitched in anticipation. But he was not going to fuck her in the car – not with his dick, at least.

He increased his pace when Meredith's legs tightened around his waist. There were tears of pleasure at the corners of her eyes, and he knew she was close to cumming. He inserted another finger inside her pussy and pushed deeper and harder. She moaned, tugging his hair forcefully.

When she came violently, he pulled his fingers out of her and sucked and lapped at her tight hole, releasing more of her sweet juices.

She tasted too delightful for him not to enjoy every second of this.

He watched her catch her breath as he licked her pussy clean, helping her fix her outfit. He wiped away the sweat from her face and let her rest her head on his shoulders.

There was not a word spoken between them but they were both smiling.

It was the most comfortable silence he'd had.

Pulling her close, he planted a kiss on her forehead, letting her lean her head against his chest as he smelled her hair. He looked out the window, .

He hoped they could stay like that just a little while longer.

28

oday was a half day at work due to scheduling conflicts. Even Sosie was taking time off. Meredith was bored after completing her work for the day – she'd already made some calls and submitted her weekly report to Mitch ahead of schedule. She was in her room, trying to think of how she wanted to spend her valuable free time. Pacing back and forth, she was trying to decide between the gym or going out shopping.

She stopped in her tracks when there was a knock on her door, a smile escaping her lips. She was not expecting anyone other than Elijah.

"Hi," he whispered, smiling when she opened the door, making her grin in return.

"Hi," she greeted back with an idea popping in her head. "Wait there," she spoke, shutting the door.

Meredith quickly grabbed her purse, phone and sunglasses before exiting her room. Eli was standing by the elevator when she searched the hallway. It would be questionable if others saw him standing outside her room, wouldn't it?

She walked toward him while putting on her sunglasses, feeling excited more than ever. She had decided to spend the entire afternoon with him – have fun and create memories – something normal couples would do.

Pressing the button for the elevator, Elijah looked at her, clearly confused. She just nodded at him, indicating that he had to take the elevator with her.

"What are you planning?" he asked the moment the doors closed.

"Nothing," she responded with a shrug, trying to play it cool.

She was sure Elijah would never agree to her plan if she told him. She would make sure he wouldn't get a chance to turn her down. He was going with her whether he liked it or not.

When the elevator stopped at the ground floor, Meredith walked toward the exit. And Elijah followed her quietly, nodding and smiling at people who acknowledged him.She called for a taxi while searching online for the nearest arcade. She would take Elijah out to release some stress and have some fun. Not like sex wasn't good for both those things. It's just that she wanted some quality time with him without having sex for a change.

She felt her pussy clench when she thought about the other day, how he'd made her cum with just his fingers. It was the wildest and naughtiest thing she'd done so far, getting fucked inside a moving car. She never thought she'd be daring enough to do such a thing.

But she had – and with Elijah Scott.

With the man who rendered her defenseless each time he touched her.

When Elijah got in the cab, she told the driver the address for the arcade. She was excited as her eyes wandered over the busy streets.

"Where are we going?" he asked, breaking the silence.

"An arcade," she answered.

"For what?" he questioned, his forehead creased.

"To have a little fun."

"Am I not enough?" he said playfully, giving her left leg a squeeze.

"I meant outdoors," she said, rolling her eyes. She was hoping he wouldn't fight her on this when he left out a soft chuckle.

"Alright," he agreed, much to her surprise. "My time is yours."

"Thank you," she murmured when she felt his fingers intertwine with hers. His touch was warm and reassuring, making her feel more relaxed as they traveled in silence.

After a good fifteen minutes, they arrived at the crowded arcade. Her heart skipped a beat when she saw the go-karts. She went to the booth to buy tickets immediately. That was the first thing she wanted to do together.

She could see Elijah shaking his head, but she didn't mind. They were there to have some fun.

"No wonder Ellie likes you," she heard him commenting as they got in their own karts. They raced, and she laughed heartily when Elijah was having a hard time maneuvering his ride. He looked awkward because of his tall frame.

For the first time, she saw him genuinely laughing and enjoying himself. She watched him smile, wishing he would smile more often like that.

"I'm tired," he shouted, finally giving up the cramped space of his kart.

"Let's have a match, then," she urged, looking at the air hockey table.

"Game," he spoke, accepting the challenge as they got off the go-karts.

After buying tickets, they went straight to their assigned table and started a fierce competition. The game was getting intense, so she thought she'd talk about something to lift the competitive air between them.

She pursed her lips, stealing a glance at him.

"Can I ask you something?" she asked, biting her lower lip.

"Ask away," he answered with a smile on his lips, not sparing her a glance as he focused on the puck.

Meredith swallowed as she mustered all her courage.

"Do you have plans to get married?" she inquired, looking away when he shot up straight in surprise, missing the puck that was whizzing by.

"What makes you ask?"

"I'm just curious," she spoke innocently, shrugging.

"What about you?" he shot back instead.

"No. Not yet. But I still have plenty of time to figure that out," she answered.

She was only interested in getting married to Elijah, of course.

But she didn't want to scare him away by saying that.

He smirked. "Gotcha," he muttered.

Finally getting bored of the game, they went to the batting cages. The competitiveness between them just a couple of minutes ago completely vanished as the conversation turned into something deeper and serious.

Meredith lined up behind the plate, waiting for the pitch.

"Is not getting married a dealbreaker for you?" he asked just as she was about to swing.

It had been ages since she'd gone to the batting cages, but she thought she'd try her best to hit at least one or two. When the whizzing ball flew from the machine, she swallowed hard and swung her body, hitting it with her metal bat.

She still had it.

"Long-term?" she asked, glancing up at him. "Yeah, that would be a dealbreaker."

"What about short-term?" he probed.

She shrugged, waiting for another ball.

"I don't know. Maybe if I knew there was a ring waiting for me in the future," she answered, chuckling softly at the hilarity of her statement.

"Would you… would you consider keeping a relationship low-key if you knew that it would be rewarding eventually?" he asked hesitantly, making her stand up straight.

Meredith's turned to look at him, completely missing the ball.

"Is that your way of asking if I'm willing to be your secret girlfriend, Elijah?"

He fell silent for a moment and averted his gaze.

"Maybe."

Feeling insulted, she let go of the bat and pulled the helmet off her head. She had never dreamed of getting involved into a secret love affair. She had always been patient when it came to relationships, and she knew what she deserved.

She knew her worth. And being Elijah's little secret was not something she would gladly accept. She deserved better than that.

She looked at him with a blank expression on her face. But deep inside she could feel an invisible hand squeezing her heart. She was hurt. And the pain was just too extreme for her to even cry.

She felt like she was going to vomit any moment now because of the burning sensation in her chest. It was getting harder to breathe with each second that passed, and she wasn't leaving without giving him a piece of her mind. How dare he ask her to be his dirty little secret?

But just when she was about to open her mouth and tell him off, a group of people recognized Elijah excitedly and he was pulled away to talk about the campaign, leaving her behind with a heavy heart.

Swallowing her tears, Meredith slipped out of the arcade. She was in so much pain, and she just wanted to be alone.

Expecting something good from him had been her biggest mistake. Thinking he'd be willing to go public with their relationship was nothing more than a stupid fantasy. She was an idiot for thinking her love life was some kind of fairy tale come true.

Trusting Elijah Scott with her heart had been her second mistake.

She should have known better.

Of course he'd never give up his political ambitions for her. They barely knew each other, after all.

She never should have gotten herself mixed up with him!

29

$\mathcal{E}$lijah's schedule was increasingly hectic. Instead of spending time on the road campaigning over the past week, he'd remained within D.C. and the surrounding area, attending a series of donor meetings and fundraisers. He'd barely spent any time at home. It had been over a week since going to the arcade with Meredith, and he was dying to be alone with her. But she hadn't made any effort to see him.

He knew why she was mad, and why she kept blowing him off. And he knew what he'd asked her, however indirectly, was wrong. But he didn't know what else to do. He didn't want to lose her, but he was so close to winning the election. Going public with a relationship now would kill his approval ratings.

What was even more irritating was that with Meredith making herself scarce, Sosie was back to acting like a clingy, jealous girlfriend. He was relieved when he was able to ditch her at the gala he was attending.

He looked around for Henry, and found him chatting with Meredith by the veranda. She looked stunning in a white gown that hugged her curves perfectly. Her hair was styled into a loose bun, with a few strands loose on either side of her face. He felt a pang of longing as he watched her laughing gleefully while talking with his best friend.

Walking toward them, Elijah worked hard to get his face straight. He missed her so much he thought he was going to slowly go insane. He stopped when he was just a few feet away from them.

"Eli!" Henry spoke, noticing his presence. "I was just telling her how you puked the first time you got drunk," he said with a laugh.

It had been one of the most embarrassing moments of his life. No wonder Meredith had been laughing her heart out before he'd walked over. He wanted to tell her she looked gorgeous and pull her in for a kiss, but he knew that was impossible.

Still, he thought she looked like a fucking angel in her white dress.

Henry suggested they find an empty table, and Eli hoped that Meredith would sit next to him. Instead she sat next to Henry, laughing hysterically at his jokes. Eli didn't catch any of them, because he'd been too busy staring at her.

She was the total package. Gorgeous, smart, hardworking... she deserved so much more than what he could give her.

All too soon, Meredith stood up, saying she had to leave, mentioning something about a get-together at her parents' house. She politely said her goodbyes and left.

Eli was barely able to wish her goodbye, sitting there stiffly as he watched her leave.

"Want to go for a walk?" Henry asked, looking at him like he was truly pitiful.

Nodding his head, Elijah rose from his seat and followed Henry, seeing them out of the crowded ballroom. They went down the illuminated pathway that led to the greenhouse and manmade river.

The place was gorgeous, but he couldn't enjoy the beautiful view because he was bothered by a lot of things. Plus, he didn't have the slightest idea what to do with Meredith. He didn't want everything between them to end just like that. But he didn't have a choice, did he?

"What's wrong with you?" Henry asked, and he raised his head in surprise at the hint of irritation in his friend's tone.

"What?" he asked, confused.

"You finally found yourself an amazing girl, but you're all moody. Are things that bad with the campaign?" Henry asked, kicking at a tiny rock.

Elijah took a closer look at Henry's face. The man was serious.

"No, the campaign is going great, actually," he answered.

"So what's wrong?"

He stayed quiet for a moment, staring blankly at the dark night sky filled with stars. Henry was right. Meredith was amazing. And she deserved better and more than what he could offer.

"I care about her, a lot… but I wish I could give her more," he spoke in between sighs. "There's no way she's going to stay with me as things are."

He didn't understand why, but tears started to form in his eyes. The mere thought of Meredith leaving him was tearing him apart. He wouldn't be able to bear it if he saw her with someone else.

"How things are?" Henry repeated, still puzzled.

"I'm a presidential candidate, Henry. Goddamn it! I can't exactly bring my twenty-something girlfriend out onto the stage for a kiss and expect people to applaud," he spoke while gritting his teeth as his hands clenched into fists. "My political enemies will rip her to shreds. And that's only the beginning."

"I see." Henry patted him on the shoulders while nodding his head, finally understanding what was wrong.

"I just… I know she's going to leave. And besides, I've got other things to worry about. Christ! I've got the fucking campaign to win."

"So… that's it, then?" Henry asked.

Eli wiped at a tear rolling down his left cheek.

This was the first and only time in his entire life he'd ever been scared over losing a woman. Worse, he knew he'd fucked up, and he'd never have the chance to tell her how he really felt about her. He never thought he could be in so much pain over someone he'd only known for a few months. How was this even possible?

You found love, said a voice in his head.

And this time, he didn't have a reason to disagree. What else could it be?

Yes, he loved Meredith Fields.

He was madly and infuriatingly in love with her.

"Yeah, Henry… I guess that's it," he murmured in agreement. The realization gutted him.

"How 'bout a glass of whisky?" Henry suggested.

After a moment of silence, Eli nodded his head and Henry led the way back to the large ballroom. He hoped the alcohol would help lessen the pain he was feeling. He silently wished it would help his heart grow numb.

30

*E*li and his campaign team arrived in Boston a few days after the gala in D.C. After the conversation he'd had with Henry regarding his relationship with Meredith, he was having a hard time getting to sleep – just like the other night. And he was getting more and more irritable with the slightest things – especially Sosie.

Sitting at the foot of his bed, he dialed her number as he planned to cancel all his plans for the day. He wanted some time alone for himself, to clear his mind.

"Reschedule all of my plans for today," he said the moment Sosie picked up.

"What– You can't," she answered begrudgingly. He could imagine the sour look on her face. "You can't cancel your plans for today. You're meeting–"

"If you can't, then I'll have to find someone who will," he said cutting her off, not bothering to hide his annoyance. He didn't have the patience to put up with Sosie's nagging anymore. He was just too tired of having silly arguments with her.

She gasped over the line, making him feel a pang of regret for talking to her that way. More than anyone else, he knew that Sosie was doing her job perfectly. And if it weren't for her efforts, he wouldn't be leading the polls, and the campaign wouldn't be as good as it was.

"Fine," she responded curtly, cutting the call short.

Elijah was more than happy to finally get some time to himself. When he checked his phone, he decided to attend the Navy SEAL's funeral at the last moment, locking himself in the bathroom to get a quick shower.

He had donned a black suit and sneaked out of his hotel room. As he marched through the corridors, he hesitated when he passed by Meredith's room. He found himself knocking on her door, thinking about something to say.

When he was finally able to make up his mind, she opened the door, a crack, surprised to see him. She opened the door a little wider and he found her looking beautiful as usual, dressed formally in a white blouse and black pants.

"Today's events are canceled," he informed her, looking deep into her ocean blue eyes.

"Yes, I just got Sosie's announcement. You shouldn't have bothered coming all the way here," she said coolly.

"I want you to come with me somewhere."

She bit her bottom lip, looking hesitant while looking down at her outfit. He suspected she felt self-conscious about what she was wearing.

"You're perfect," he whispered, tucking a few loose strands of hair behind her ear. "You're always perfect."

Meredith flushed but smiled at his statement, nodding her head.

"Okay, let's go."

Intertwining his fingers with hers, he led the way out of the hotel. His grip was firm, and he didn't have any intention of letting go of her hand. When she struggled to pull away from his grip as people around them watched, he only held her tighter.

Meredith shot him a confused look. Her face was beet red by the time they got in a cab. Clearly she was embarrassed with the attention they got from the people in the hotel. But he wasn't the least bit bothered by it. He just wanted to spend some time with her.

Elijah expected her to question him the moment the cab pulled away from the hotel. But she remained silent. She was just staring out the windows as they traveled to their destination. She stopped trying to pull away, and let him hold her hand.

He was glad she didn't want to talk. He didn't have any answers for her, none she would like at least. All he knew was that he wanted to be with her.

When they arrived at a cemetery, she shot him a puzzled look.

"What are we doing here?" she asked.

"We're attending a funeral."

She paused, still confused.

"Whose funeral?"

"A friend. He died while serving the country," he murmured softly.

Meredith fell silent again, regretful for asking questions. He squeezed her hand softly, reassuring her everything was fine. He was fine – because she was with him.

"I'm sorry," she said.

"You don't have to be," he said, then sighed.

He looked at the crowd of mourners. He felt incredibly guilty, watching the sobbing family members of the SEAL who had died in the strike. The outcome of which he'd altered for selfish reasons. Smiling bitterly, he uttered a silent apology.

And as much as he wanted to regret what he'd done, he didn't. That could have been his brother they were burying instead, his mother sobbing at the graveside.

It was an impossible decision to make.

But he'd done it for his family.

And he knew others in his position would have done the same. Not that it brought him any comfort.

He sighed, feeling the heavy burden even more.

"Every time I see something like this, I'm reminded how fleeting our lives are. That we should chase what we want with the time we're given. You have to do it… while you can," he said as tears formed in his eyes. He was getting all choked up with emotion.

His late father had always taught him to live life to the fullest, so he wouldn't have any regrets. Eli shook his head and clenched his jaw tightly. He was living his life the exact opposite way of his father's advice.

Life always found a way to get in between him and his dreams.

He knew happiness couldn't be achieved without sacrifice. But did he really have to sacrifice Meredith – his happiness – for his political ambition?

He felt Meredith's cool hand on his face as she looked deep into his grey eyes. It was a little difficult to make out her face because of the tears in his eyes, but he could see she was worried. She leaned in and kissed him gently on the mouth, murmuring softly about how everything would be alright.

He gathered his composure. As they got down from the cab, he held Meredith's hand and together they walked toward the funeral party.

Just for today, he thought, squeezing the hand of the woman he loved.

31

It had been several days since Meredith and Elijah had attended the funeral. Elijah had stayed busy since then, meeting with donors and campaign strategists. Meredith missed him so much. She was starting to feel like he'd completely forgotten about her.

He's worked so hard to get to this point. He can't give up now, she thought while staring blankly at the screen of her phone, wishing Lily would call her.

She was feeling restless and bored, but she couldn't find the motivation to be productive. And all she could think about was Elijah – wishing she could be with him right now, wishing he were here so they could kiss and hug and have amazing makeup sex.

She missed his touch so much. It hadn't even been a week, and she felt like she was dying without him. How was that even possible?

I'm getting more and more pathetic, she winced.

Meredith thought about how special Elijah was to her. With him, she'd done things she never thought she could do – particularly in bed. Having him around made her feel secure. He reminded her constantly how beautiful he found her.

Being with him made her feel perfect – and complete.

A knock at her door brought her back to reality. Her heart skipped a beat, hoping it would be Elijah. She almost couldn't believe it when she saw him standing outside her door.

"Hi," he said huskily.

God, how she'd missed him awkwardly saying that word!

"Hi," she replied.

"Look, I just want to tell you that I'm so sorry," he mumbled softly, looking at the floor.

Meredith's face fell.

"What do you mean?" she asked, confused.

Without saying anything else, Elijah stepped inside her room, locking the door behind him. He pulled her into a deep and long kiss. She was surprised at first, but she soon relaxed against him. She'd been longing for his touch for so long.

And now, she was finally back in his arms.

Elijah's embrace was growing tighter, making her squirm uncomfortably. He was making it hard for her to breathe.

"You're going to kill me, Eli," she whispered, breaking their kiss, trying to pull away from his grasp.

"I'm so sorry for not spending time with you lately," he whispered, his voice cracking.

And for the first time in a while, she felt like she was going to melt. She was totally aware of Eli's responsibilities and plans. And she wasn't expecting him to apologize like he was afraid of losing her.

Speechless, Meredith found her mouth being devoured with intense softness. There was longing and sincerity with the way he moved, making her respond with the same intensity.She was growing hot as he brushed a hand down her hair. But he stopped kissing her, pulling away.

"What is it?" she blurted, annoyed.

A mischievous smile flashed on Elijah's gorgeous face before walking away to pull down the blinds and close the curtains of her room.

Licking her lips, she walked toward him and jumped into his arms, wrapping her legs around his body. She planted a kiss on the tip of his nose. She didn't care about anything else, not now. All she knew was that she'd missed him terribly, and she wanted him to fuck her right here.

Meredith smiled when he pulled her body closer to his, squeezing her ass.

She broke contact for a moment, stripping naked and leaving her body free for his hands to explore. It didn't take long before he started squeezing and cupping her breasts. His mouth moved from her collarbone to a pebbled nipple, making her gasp in pleasure.

"Oh, god!" she moaned, combing her fingers through his dark locks, tugging on his head.

Impatiently, she tried to unbuckle his belt so she could get him inside her as soon as possible.

"Someone's missed me," he teased, unfastening his belt when she struggled to remove it.

"Anyone would grow impatient after waiting for so long," she answered with a frown.

She unzipped his pants and freed him from his boxers.

"Someone's missed me," she said sexily as she watched him grow in her hands while stroking him up and down. She moaned when she sat down on his lap, lining him up with her wet entrance.

But Elijah suddenly lifted her up, standing up and making her pout with frustration. She watched him remove the rest of his clothing, revealing his chiseled body.

She groaned as she moved to the bed.He crawled over her, his hands spreading her thighs wide as he placed his cock between her velvety wet folds.

"Oh, god…" she moaned against his mouth.

When she tried to wrap her arms around his neck, he caught her hands, intertwining his fingers with his, holding them above her head. She bit her lower lip in anticipation as her body hummed with excitement and need.

He teased her slowly and deliberately with the head of his cock, rubbing it back and forth over her hard clit, but refusing to enter her even as she bucked her hips. She thought she was going to go insane if he didn't fuck her soon.

She thrashed her head on the bed, begging him to continue but he rocked against her, sending shivers up her spine.

"Ohhhh…" she whispered as he kissed her roughly, biting her bottom lip and groaning into his mouth.

Meredith gasped as he filled her in one fluid thrust without warning her beforehand. She screamed with pleasure as he pounded her pussy.

She could already feel her walls quivering around him as he slid in and out of her faster and deeper. He kissed her and she began to feel the telltale flutters of her release.

"Yes! Yes, yes, yes," she cried as her legs locked even tighter around his waist.

Elijah took her lips in a passionate kiss as he claimed her body, driving her to her climax before he himself reached his peak.

He moaned into her mouth as he shot his load, muscles tightening and heart racing.

Meredith stroked his back with one hand whilst the other played with his hair as they lay together, catching their breath – and maybe preparing for another round.

After a couple of minutes, her phone started ringing. She silenced it without looking at the caller ID, wanting to enjoy more time with Elijah. She wanted to make the best of it while she still could. She wouldn't know when they'd be together next.

She wouldn't let anyone disturb them.

"It's okay. Take it," Elijah whispered before planting a kiss on her temple.

Obligingly, she answered the call with a furrowed brow. It was an unregistered caller.

"Hello?" she spoke, glancing at Elijah who was also curious who was calling.

"This is Vernice from Marie Claire. Is this Meredith Fields?" Her heart skipped a beat.

Someone from Marie Claire was calling her!

Eyeing Elijah, she grabbed her robe and went out onto the terrace. She wasn't expecting to get a call from someone as big as Marie Claire.

"Speaking. What made you call?" she asked, wincing when she realized she sounded too casual.

"I'm an editor from Marie Claire, and I've been enjoying the stuff you've been writing for the paper. I'm very interested in sitting down with you and talking about your next move," Vernice said.

Meredith blinked in surprise. Had she just gotten an offer from one of the biggest fashion and lifestyle magazines in the world?

She swallowed, struggling for words.

"I'll be on the road for the next three weeks, at least… or maybe more," she answered, stealing glances at Elijah who was starting to get dressed.

Vernice chuckled.

"Yeah, I know. I'd be very delighted to see you when you get back to New York."

Biting her lip, she looked at Eli who was already standing in front of her, fully dressed. He looked pensive.

"Sure. I'll get in touch once I'm off the road," she said, which Vernice gladly agreed to.

When the phone call ended, Eli asked her who it was, looking curious more than ever when she averted her gaze. She didn't want him to think that she was leaving the campaign.

No. She didn't want to leave the campaign.

She wanted to stay with him until the election.

"Someone from Marie Claire," she answered softly, walking past him and sitting at the foot of the bed. "But I don't think I'm going to call them back," she added, fidgeting with her fingernails.

She sighed.

It was a huge opportunity. But she felt like things were going too fast for her career. She wanted to take things easy. And enjoy what she currently had… Elijah.

Meredith raised her head when she saw Elijah's feet in front of hers. He wasn't stupid, and telling him that it was nothing would be ridiculous.

"Why not?" he asked with narrowed eyes, unconvinced.

"It's just… nothing."

"They called you for nothing?"

"It's nothing important, okay? I'm going to the gym," she snapped. Her thoughts were still a jumbled mess.

She didn't mean to sound so bitchy. But she didn't know how to handle the situation. And she didn't want Eli to think she was turning down a brilliant opportunity just because of him.

"I trust you can see yourself out," she said quietly, gathering her gym clothes, locking herself in the bathroom.

She needed some time alone to clear her head and organize her thoughts.

She needed to think.

32

*E*lijah couldn't understand why Meredith would turn down an offer from a company as big as Marie Claire. When she snapped at him, he knew that the job was something she really wanted.

It was something she'd been looking forward to for a very long time.

He didn't want to get ahead of himself, but he had a feeling that it was all because of him. And her relationship with him was the biggest factor in why she declined the offer. He didn't want her to lose opportunities because of him. He wasn't willing to give up his career just to be with her.

At least, he thought he wasn't.

"I don't want you to lose something as big as this, Meredith. I want you to reconsider your decision. I don't want to get in between you and your dreams."

She scoffed.

"Don't get ahead of yourself, Elijah. I'm not turning it down because of you. The decision is for me to make. You don't have anything to do with it. Besides, did you ever consider me when you're making decisions?" she barked angrily, planting her hands on her hips.

She was deadly serious.

Eli fell silent.

"Oh, why did I even bother to ask the obvious? Of course you don't. Your ambition is a whole different thing. And you're not even taking our relationship into account," she smirked, then shrugged. "If you can even call this a relationship," she muttered under her breath.

He stayed quiet and looked at her. He knew that she was thinking about it all along. But he didn't expect that he'd be speechless the moment she'd bring up the topic. It was hard to answer or even deny. Because everything she said was true.

Gritting his teeth, his hands balled into fists. Although he knew he was in the wrong, he was hurt. He was just trying to make her see the possibilities of a brilliant career ahead of her. He only wanted her to pursue what she wanted to do.

But maybe it was a wrong move.

"Fine! Do whatever you want. And you can't ever put anything that happened tonight in print," he spoke coldly.

It was their very first fight. And he didn't want her to take it to heart. He was afraid that everything would change because of the damned argument. If possible, he just wanted them to forget about it.

Meredith let out a dry laugh. Her face turned red, as well as the tips of her ears. She folded her arms over her chest. She looked insulted.

"I thought you trusted me. All this time, you've been thinking I'd break my promise to you just to get back at you? You disgust me!" she shouted at the top of her lungs.

"You're acting like a spoiled brat. You think everything should go your way because you've had everything handed to you on a silver fucking platter your entire life. That's not how the real world works, Meredith," he growled. He could see she was angry, but he couldn't stop himself from adding the next part.

"But what can I do? You're just a little girl. You don't understand anything," he said, shrugging for a more sarcastic effect.

Her eyes widened. Maybe he'd gone too far.

Pursing her lips, she met his gaze with the same intensity of anger. She didn't look the least bit intimidated with his stares, or scared of his aura. She was undaunted as she filled her chest with air and released a heavy breath.

"I can understand you perfectly when we're fucking each other. Things are crystal clear then. But I couldn't understand the relationship between us, no matter how hard I tried," she grumbled. She paused, then scoffed. "But I guess I understand it now."

Eli watched as her eyes filled with tears, and it broke his heart when a tear rolled down her cheek. He hadn't wanted to hurt her. He never meant to.

And he didn't want to see her cry.

He reached out to wipe away her tears, but she jerked away from him like she'd been burned. Rubbing at her face, she shot him a look of utter contempt and disgust. That was when he realized the words he'd spoken had been more than enough to break their bond.

He never should have called her a spoiled brat, because she wasn't, not really. And saying that she didn't understand anything had just been cruel.

Meredith may be young, but she was undeniably brilliant.

Her intelligence made her sexier than any of the women he'd known in his past.

She was everything he wanted.

No.

She was all he wanted.

But it seemed like he'd be losing her for good after this. It was all so stupid.

"I didn't mea–"

"This is just another fling. I'm just one of those women for you," she spoke in almost a whisper, tears flowing freely down her cheeks.

Elijah struggled for the right words to say to put her at ease, but his mind felt like it was shutting down entirely as he watched her.

He'd already made up his mind – he couldn't quit his political ambitions, and he was willing to give up the happiness he'd found with Meredith. Arguing with her and insisting she was more than a fling would just be giving her false hope at this point.

Even though for him, she wasn't just a fling.

She was one in a million.

And even though their time together was short and fleeting, she'd given him a glimpse of real happiness. He'd always cherish the memories they'd made together.

He fought the urge to pull her close for a hug. He wanted nothing more than to embrace her tightly, soothe away her pains, and reassure her that he would stay by her side no matter what.

But he knew he couldn't do that.

She shot him a disappointed glare before storming out of his room without sparing him another glance.

She was badly hurt, he could tell. But things were better this way.

33

After the fight with Elijah, Meredith spent the remaining weeks of the final campaign push working her ass off in order to get him out of her mind.

She missed him so badly.

But she couldn't stop obsessing over the things he'd said to her.

She'd thought Elijah was different. That her family's wealth and status didn't matter to him. After the times they'd spent together and the conversations they'd had, she'd thought he'd understood her. Come to find out, he hadn't really understood her at all.

She'd been deeply hurt because she wasn't like that.

She was grateful for what she had, and worked hard not to come across as a spoiled princess.

But the absolute worst was when he'd just gone along with what she'd said about just being another one of his flings. Deep down, she'd wanted him to comfort her and tell her she was more than that. That she was special, and that he really liked her.

And maybe…

Just maybe, things would have turned out a lot better if he'd just told her he loved her.

Because she knew…

She'd fallen in love with him, hard and fast.

It was like she was falling into a bottomless pit – there was no end to it.

Knocking back a shot of whisky, Meredith smiled bitterly, thinking that it was definitely for the best that Elijah hadn't bothered to chase her. The last thing she needed was him getting her hopes up for the millionth time.

Now she knew not to expect anything from him. He'd made it crystal clear that she was nothing more than a fling, a toy used to kill time and relieve his sexual frustrations. She was just the latest in a long line of women who'd fallen for his charms.

"Meredith," she heard her mother calling out her name.

It was a few nights before Election Day, and she was finally back at home, currently drinking herself silly. She should have been spending time bonding with her family. But her mind was filled with thoughts of nothing but Elijah, as usual.

She did a double take when her mother came close.

Her mom was drunk. It had been awhile since she'd seen her like this.

She looked for her father, but he was already passed out on the couch. He'd never been much of a drinker, not like her mother.

Bonnie was traveling with friends.

She sighed, wishing that her little sister was there. At least she'd have someone to talk with.

"Mom, you're drunk," she spoke softly, filling her glass with more whisky.

"I-I-I'm not," Elizabeth argued, stuttering. "Just tipsy."

Rolling her eyes, Meredith chuckled.

"Whatever," she said, not wanting to argue. "Come on, let's get you to bed."

"No," her mother protested, shaking her head.

Meredith fought the urge to laugh. Who would have ever thought that the Elizabeth Howard Fields would be like this when drunk?

I took after her, I guess.

"D-Do you know what I have always dreamt for you and your sister?" Elizabeth spoke gently, her expression soft like she was thinking about something very beautiful.

Her mother was usually an emotionally messy drunk, laughing until she cried, or singing until she'd lose her voice. But right now she was acting differently, making Meredith feel anxious.

"What is it?" she asked hesitantly.

Her mother smiled bitterly, with a single tear rolling down her left cheek.

Meredith held her breath. Had her mother gone senile?

"I want the two of you to marry someone you love and who could love you the same way," Elizabeth responded emotionally. "I don't want you to be in a loveless marriage for convenience."

She stayed quiet, studying her mother's expression a little bit longer. Her mother didn't sound like she was joking, and she knew it was the heaviest burden she'd been carrying in her heart for a long time.

Meredith was aware of what her mom was referring to, of course. But she hadn't expected her mother to ever openly talk about it.

But maybe tonight, she thought her mother would open up.

"Nobody wants a marriage without love, Mom. It'll never last without love," she said bitterly.

Just like her relationship with Elijah. Her love for him was completely one-sided. The only feeling shared between them was lust, pure and simple.

Elizabeth smiled. "You're right."

She fell silent, but she longed to ask her mother a very specific question. It was the same question she'd always wanted to ask her parents, but had never had the guts to discuss. But maybe now was the right time.

"But you and dad have been together for more than two decades. So I guess it could work," she said delicately, hinting around the issue. "You had me, then Bonnie."

"I love your dad, Mer," Elizabeth blurted.

Meredith froze.

"I agreed to marry him because I love him. But his heart belonged to someone else," her mother confessed, her cheeks flooded with tears.

Meredith didn't know how to react at this sudden revelation.

Her heart ached for her mom. How could she have possibly endured this for so long all by herself?

"I had no idea," she whispered, hugging her mom fiercely, hoping it would soothe her at least a little bit.

More than ever, she felt blessed. Because of her mother's patience and sacrifice, she'd been able to grow up with a complete family. She may not have been the best daughter, but she'd grown up to be a good person thanks to her parents.

"Mom?" she prompted when Elizabeth's sobs turned faint.

"Hmmm…?"

"What if I was in a secret relationship? One that no one knew about, but I was happy."

"Well… it's not a relationship if you can't tell your parents about it, is it?"

Meredith shook her head glumly. She cared about Elijah, there was no denying that. She was certain that she loved him.

But her mom and Lily were right. She wasn't some dirty little secret. And it didn't matter if there was a ten year difference between them. If she was going to be in a relationship with him, she wanted the whole package.

She wouldn't accept less.

Because that was what she deserved.

34

After mulling things over, Meredith sobered up and decided she and Eli needed to talk. She didn't want things between them to end the way they had. Plus she felt she deserved to know what she really meant to him. She'd ask him face to face, and she'd accept whatever his answer would be.

It was possible he would break her heart all over again, but at least this way she wouldn't be left wondering about all the what ifs she couldn't stop thinking about.

During the drive, she thought long and hard about the questions she wanted to ask him. It would be best to be prepared. She just hoped she could remain calm.

Just the idea of asking him about his feelings was starting to make her feel anxious. But she knew she needed to make the first move.

She didn't want to have any regrets, come what may.

And if the worst came to pass, it'd be best for her to hear it directly from him, so she could start moving on with her life.

After parking her car in front of Eli's house, she ran through the same breathing exercises she'd used to help calm herself down the night of the party. The night where it had all started, for better or for worse. She didn't bother looking in the mirror. She wasn't there to impress him, after all.

She just needed some answers. That's it.

She got out of her car and quickly walked to his front door, knocking three times. She knew it was late, and him not being home or asleep were both very real possibilities. But she still had to try.

After a few moments, she knocked again. But there was no answer.

Biting her lip, she tested the knob and was surprised when she learned the door was unlocked. Without hesitating, she walked inside and looked around the living room and kitchen. Still, there was no trace of Elijah.

Meredith decided to go to the pool area where the party had been held the last time she'd been at his house. The lights were on, making her feel certain that Elijah was still awake and that he was somewhere on the patio.

When she reached the slightly opened glass sliding door leading to the pool area, she saw him leaning against a wooden chair. He was talking with Sosie, but she couldn't see their faces because of the angle.

Just after she took a step closer, Elijah held Sosie's hand in the air, leaning closer – kissing her. Meredith wasn't sure what they were doing, but she was certain that whatever was happening wasn't good for her heart.

She covered her mouth with a hand to suppress the gasp that was trying to escape, her knees growing weak as she stared at them. Elijah was kissing Sosie!

She was not expecting to see that.

Tears welled in her eyes as she struggled for air. She could feel a piercing pain in her heart, as if a thousand tiny needles were pricking it repeatedly.

She was feeling an unimaginable pain she'd never experienced before.

God, she was so stupid! He'd already made it clear she was nothing more than a fling. Talking wouldn't change that. What had she been thinking, barging into his house like she had any kind of right to be there?

She needed to get out of here before they saw her. She didn't think she could deal with Sosie right now, let alone Elijah after what she'd just witnessed.

Turning on her heels, she accidentally bumped into a table in her haste, knocking a large decorative vase to the floor, where it shattered.

She stared stupidly at the broken pieces of glass for a split second before she quickly ran away without looking back.

She never should have gone there.

It was a mistake.She didn't know how she'd made it out of his house without being discovered, but the next thing she knew she was already inside her car, starting the engine and pulling away.

Damn you, Elijah Scott! she cursed silently, as tears continued to fall down her cheeks.

35

*E*lijah was shocked to see Meredith standing by the door. One hand covered her mouth and her eyes were wide, making him realize she was probably thinking he'd made a move on Sosie.

Fuck!

Without saying a word, he shoved Sosie away, taking quick footsteps to follow Meredith who was running away like she was scared of him. He wanted to tell her that what she was thinking was wrong.

He didn't want her to think that he was doing just fine without her. Or that he was having fun with someone new. Because neither of those things were even remotely true.

He wanted to talk to her and tell her what she really meant to him. He wanted to hug her, and kiss her. He wanted to make things right between them.

But Meredith was growing more and more distant, and he couldn't blame her.

After the argument they'd had, it would be a miracle if she forgave him. He'd said awful things he couldn't take back.

And now, she'd misunderstood what she'd seen. Sosie had been lecturing him about the campaign, as usual. And he'd gotten pissed off when she started pointing her fingers in his face. So he'd gripped her arm to prevent her from doing that while Sosie snarled at him. From Meredith's vantage point it must have looked like he'd been getting ready to hook up with Sosie.

Fuck.

"Meredith," he called out, but she didn't stop. She just continued running until she reached her car.

Please hear me out, he murmured to himself as he watched her drive away, leaving him in the driveway. What did I do to deserve this kind of torture?

Gritting his teeth, he marched back inside the house then punched the first thing that caught his eye – a vase identical to the one Meredith had broke. He was mad for not being able to tell her what he wanted to say. He was mad at himself for being such a coward.

"Let her be," he heard Sosie mutter from the far corner of the living room, making him grow even angrier.

If it wasn't for her, he would probably be having a calm conversation with Meredith right now. If it wasn't for her, Meredith wouldn't have gotten the wrong idea.

"Shut up!"

Sosie narrowed her eyes. She looked pissed..

"Don't tell me you're in love with her," she sneered.

Eli didn't bother to reply, because he knew his face was giving away how he truly felt.

He was in love with Meredith.

"Answer me, Elijah!" Sosie yelled from across the room. Her normally cool and collected demeanor was totally ruined as her hands clenched into tight fists.

Eli felt guilty when he saw tears streaming down Sosie's face. For a long time, he'd known about her feelings toward him. And he'd thought it wouldn't be so bad to date her after the election, until Meredith showed up, turning his world upside down.

"I'm sorry," he said. He didn't know what else to say.

"You idiot! You're risking your chances of winning the election for some... little girl!" she screamed angrily, biting her lips. He wasn't sure, but he thought he saw a drop of blood on her lower lip.

Pinching the bridge of his nose, he closed his eyes, trying to calm himself.

"Maybe I care about Meredith more than winning," he spoke softly, then smiled bitterly. It had taken him far too long to understand what was more important to him.

"Would that be so bad?" he added, looking at Sosie who had gone red.

She walked up to him, gritting her teeth in anger.

"You made a mistake choosing her over me, Elijah," she hissed, pointing a finger in his face. "You'll regret it."

With that, Sosie stormed out of his house, her heels rapidly clicking on the concrete.

Feeling drained, he sank to the floor, feeling completely hopeless. He didn't know what to do, and he didn't think her parents would appreciate it very much if he just showed up at Meredith's house. He wasn't sure what he would say, or how he would even start talking to her.

Is this the end of everything?

$\mathcal{M}$eredith slowly opened her eyes when she felt someone shaking her awake. Rubbing at her eyelids, she realized it was Bonnie. She sat up in bed with a smile, happy as always to see her little sister.

"Hey, I didn't know you would be back from your trip today," she murmured then yawned, pressing a hand over her mouth.

"Yeah, well. The election's in a few days and Brittany's father said she had to be back by today and she was the one driving, so…"

Meredith groaned.

"Jesus! You're right. I wish I could just… sleep until it's all over," she grumbled, pulling a pillow over her face.

She didn't want to hear anything about the election. She was so fucking nervous about the results. If only they could just fast forward to the end already.

"Well, you'd better check out today's news. You feature prominently in the headline," Bonnie mumbled, flipping the pages of the paper deliberately for her to hear.

Jumping out of bed, she raced over to Bonnie and snatched the copy of the paper out of her hands before flopping back onto her bed. Meredith's eyes widened when she saw a photo of Eli splashed across the front page, along with her senior photo from her high school yearbook in the corner. The headline read, WANNABE PREZ HAS AFFAIR WITH YOUNG REPORTER.

She felt like she'd been doused with ice cold water.

Not really knowing how to react, Meredith placed a hand over her mouth, looking at Bonnie – asking for help. What was she supposed to do?

"Oh my god…" she whispered as her heart thudded painfully against her ribcage.

Her parents were going to kill her.

"Mom and Dad haven't found out yet, but they will soon," Bonnie said with an apologetic expression on her face.

"Oh, god," she whispered again, still at a loss for words.

"Yeah. I thought I should wake you up before they did… give you a chance to sneak out." Bonnie shot her a worried look, then nodded her head as if she completely understood her situation.

Instantly, Meredith found herself pulling her sister close for a tight hug. She then kissed her on the cheek before getting to her feet.

"Thank you," she muttered gratefully before quickly grabbing a bag and throwing the essentials inside - a couple of changes of clothes, her laptop, cellphone and wallet. She splashed her face with water and hurriedly got dressed, making sure to grab a pair of oversized sunglasses and a ball cap.

She had to make sure nobody recognized her, or she'd be mobbed by the press before she could even think properly.

After saying goodbye to Bonnie, she slipped out of the mansion and drove away in her car, taking an alternate route only her family and the staff knew about. She managed to avoid the press entirely, but she wanted to vomit when she saw how many people were already camped out in front of her house.

When she was out of the subdivision, she pulled into a parking garage and checked her phone, only to find missed calls from Eli, Lily, Sosie, and all the other reporters from the campaign. Cursing, she dialed Eli first. She wanted to know who'd broken the story to the media.

And she wanted to know how he was handling the scandal.

After a few rings, he picked up, which made her feel relieved at least.

"Meredith," she heard Sosie say instead, making her heart sink. Why was Sosie answering Eli's phone?

She felt a surge of jealousy as she was suddenly reminded of what she had seen between them the other night. But that wasn't the point. She had to talk to Eli.

"Umm… Hi, Sosie," she said awkwardly.

"You shouldn't be calling this number," Sosie replied, and her dislike was obvious by her tone.

"I… It's Eli's phone. Why are you answering it?" she questioned, unable to hold back any longer. She was really getting on her nerves.

"He called me when this shitstorm hit the internet last night. Someone needs to handle this mess," Sosie responded flatly.

Meredith breathed in to control her temper, her grip on the steering wheel growing tighter. She swore she'd really give Sosie a piece of her mind when everything was over. She'd just been holding back until now because they were working together on the campaign with her.

"Can I talk to him?"

Sosie scoffed, and she could picture the disdainful look on the woman's stern face.

"You cannot even begin to understand how far away from him you need to stay away. Like, permanently," Sosie answered in a warning tone.

But she wasn't going to let it end like that. She needed to talk to him.

"If I could just talk to him—"

"Yeah, no. He does *not* want to talk to you. He wants nothing to do with his dirty little secret. And a little piece of advice? Don't talk to the press. You should know – you're one of them. You guys are like vultures," Sosie said disgustedly.

"Sosie, please—"

"Gotta go, Meredith. CNN is calling."

With that, the line went dead, leaving Meredith to stare blankly at her phone.

Her face was in the paper, and now she was laying low as if she was a criminal. Worse, she wasn't even allowed to talk to Elijah! Just what the hell was happening?

Punching her dashboard, she screamed, letting out her frustrations before she got back on the road. She'd missed her chance to make things right with Eli. Now it was too late.

Everything was ruined.

Gripping the wheel, she decided that finding a place to stay was her first priority. She needed to head somewhere far from the city – where people would barely recognize her.

She would deal with things once her mind cleared up.

---

*E*lijah rushed to get inside his SUV, ignoring the swarm of reporters all thrusting microphones into his face and shouting questions regarding his affair with Meredith Fields. He was exhausted, and all he wanted to do was see and talk to Meredith.

But he couldn't afford to do that.

He didn't want to make things worse for her. He'd heard she'd left her parents' house early this morning and gone into hiding somewhere.

Plus, he was worried about what her father would do to her.

When the car pulled away from the curb, he looked at Sosie, who was busy checking her phone. It was evident that she was repressing a self-satisfied smirk.

Clenching his hands, he looked away with his jaw tensed. He awoke late last night to a story about him and Meredith coming up as an alert on his phone. At first, he thought that Sosie was behind it. But when he burst into her hotel room, she was fast asleep and as confused as anyone.

With twenty minutes until the press descended on him, he decided that it didn't matter whether or not Sosie had planted the story. He needed someone to spin this for him.

And Sosie was the only person who could do that.

Looking out the window, he wondered where Meredith was. She must have been a complete mess. The news was everywhere. Press were still camped outside her house, going crazy whenever someone came or went. Still, there was no sign of Meredith.

He was so worried.

If he could only talk to her…

Election Day was almost here, and for once, he couldn't care less about the results. All he knew was that he wanted to see Meredith safe and sound.

"I'm done with campaigning," he spoke, glancing at Sosie again.

"You'll be on CNN and MSNBC, and then we'll make a stop where you shake hands…"

"No. I'm done," he stated firmly, cutting her off as she started scrolling through notes on her phone.

Sosie shot him a defiant glare.

"You've worked so hard to get here. You deserve to be president, Elijah. Hell, if you aren't president, who's going to look out for soldiers like your brother?"

His jaw tensed as he gritted his teeth, unable to argue with the woman's remarks. But damn her for being so honest about things!

"I want you to bring Meredith here. I need to know she's okay," he muttered helplessly.

"You need to look out for your own interests first. The election is in two days. After the election, you can do whatever you want."

He smiled bitterly, then frowned. "If I lose, you mean."

"No, I didn't mean that," Sosie said defensively.

"If I win the election, it'll be a miracle. And then everyone will be so busy gearing up for the White House, romance will be pushed aside until god knows when," he said sarcastically while shaking his head.

Sosie scowled, but after a moment she cleared her throat.

"Well, I won't lie. I certainly hope that you do win. For a thousand reasons."

With an eyebrow raised, he looked out the window, stewing.

38

---

eredith woke up with a heavy heart the following morning. She didn't have the slightest idea what to do with her life now that she was trying to avoid the media. She wished all of it was just a dream.

Rolling over to one side of the bed, she suddenly felt that she wasn't alone in the room.. Startled, she sat up, and saw Bonnie and Lily staring at her.

Meredith groaned, wanting to think that this had all been some nightmare and soon she'd wake up.. The mere sight of Bonnie and Lily reminded her that she was in a hotel in the suburbs, desperately trying to escape the commotion back home.

"What a nice way to greet a friend who's traveled around the globe just to see you," Lily said.

Meredith pursed her lips, got up, and hugged her best friend. Tears started forming in her eyes as she sighed on Lily's shoulder. She was happy and relieved. She'd been starting to think that she was alone, and had forgotten about her best friend who was always willing to help..

"It's going to be okay," Lily said."How do you know? This isn't exactly like when our friends broke up in college. This is a huge scandal." Meredith was not the least bit enthusiastic about arguing with Lily.

While Bonnie called for room service to get breakfast, Meredith washed up to feel a little better. At least, she wasn't going to eat alone now that she had her sister and best friend with her.

She was still blessed, after all.

While enjoying breakfast, Lily and Bonnie pestered her to tell them everything about her and Elijah. And she was more than willing to tell her story. She just missed him so bad, to the point where she thought it wouldn't be so bad to spill all the beans now that everything was out in the open.

"Did you call him?" Bonnie asked. She sipped water from her glass.

"I did. But his campaign manager answered the call. She said he wants nothing to do with me," Meredith responded glumly, taking a bite of bacon.

Lily let out an exasperated sigh.

"Do you love him?"

Meredith fell silent as she played with the sliced tomato on her plate, wondering what to say. She thought they'd find it stupid if she said that she's in love with a man she just met two months ago.

"Meredith?" Bonnie prompted.

"Do you?" Lily asked again.

With pursed lips, she nodded her head in hesitation. There was no point in denying it when Lily and Bonnie knew her like the back of their hands. And she'd never been good at lying anyway.

She felt Lily squeezing her hand, reassuring her that it was okay.

"Do you think he feels the same?" Bonnie asked curiously.

"I don't know. I'm not sure," she spoke in almost a whisper as the memory of Elijah making a move on Sosie the night she went to his house flashed through her head.

Up until now, she'd still been trying to convince herself that her eyes were just playing a trick on her that night. Despite the fact that they'd fought over the most trivial thing – about her being just another fling – she could feel the sincerity in Elijah's words.

She knew that he really cared about her. And if she could only get one more chance to ask him, she wouldn't hesitate. But as things were, it would be impossible.

She needed to stay as far away from him as possible.

"Oh," Bonnie and Lily chorused, making her smile.

"C'mon guys, it wasn't that bad," she spoke softly. "I mean, I was happy when we were together even though it was just for a short time. And I really enjoyed it…"

Meredith wiggled her brows, making a naughty expression on her face, knowing that it was the best way to lighten the mood of their conversation. She was relieved that her sister and Lily were by her side. She didn't want them to get dragged into her pitiful situation.

"Did you really?" Bonnie asked, wide-eyed. That made her laugh for the first time in days.

Just like her, Bonnie believed that giving up her virginity was a serious thing and that her first time should be with someone special. It should be memorable.

"Of course! He's hot!" Meredith replied, piercing the last piece of sliced tomato.

"Looks like someone's going to get naughtier," Lily said giggling while shaking her head. "Don't worry, you'll forget about him after a couple of yacht parties. You got me."

Meredith leaned in to hug Lily as tears started welling in her eyes. She wanted to get away from all the stress. But she didn't think she was ready to forget about Elijah.

But she had to…

Maybe going back to her original plan for the summer – spending a year partying – would be a good start to forget about the things she didn't want to think about.

And maybe, she could fall in love with someone else, too.

39

It was late, and Meredith would be flying with Lily to Ibiza to get away from all the reporters. She'd called her parents and reassured them that she was just doing fine. And that she'd call them more often using Lily's phone.

She sighed, staring blankly at the plane that was waiting on the tarmac.

It'd been days, and Lily had made her promise to never check the internet. They'd been on media lockdown – no phones, no internet, no social networks, no data whatsoever. It was Election Day and she was dying to know the results, but she was sticking to Lily's rules.

She had to do it because she believed it was the best thing to do.

Wearing sunglasses and a cap, she gritted her teeth as anxiety devoured her.Lily handed Meredith a bag of gummy bears, which was usually an effective distraction.

But she found them unappealing this time. Meredith grimaced and shook her head.

"Nah, thanks," she murmured apologetically.

"It's going to be okay, Mer. We'll meet a lot of hot guys. You know, I heard Ibiza was a whole lot better than Bali. And I'm telling you, Bali is crazy. Imagine Ibiza!" Lily screeched excitedly.

She tried to smile, but not hard enough to actually make it happen.

She didn't want to spoil Lily's excitement, but she just couldn't feel it herself. She was about to leave everyone and everything she knew. She'd be leaving the one man she loved.

Meredith and Lily fell in line when the gate called them to board for first class. Every step felt like she was walking on a pile of nails.

"Relax, it's going to be okay. You'll be okay," she heard Lily whisper.

"Yeah," she agreed, releasing an exasperated sigh and hoping to placate her friend.

When they boarded the plane, she noticed that several flight attendants were pointing and smiling at her. Her stomach plummeted, and her cheeks reddened in embarrassment. She pulled her cap lower and bit her lip, hoping that they would stop acting rude.

She felt a light squeeze on her shoulder.

It was Lily, smiling at her.

"None of this will matter anymore once we get there," she said, fixing her seatbelt the moment they settled in their seats.

"Yeah, I know." Meredith couldn't stop the tears that began to well up in her eyes..

She wanted to slap herself in the face for feeling so emotional. It wasn't like she was going away forever. It was just for a couple of months.

Lowering her head to hide her tears, she grabbed a magazine and started flipping through the pages. She could hear passengers getting onboard, filling the plane. She was not in the mood to talk when a flight attendant walked up to her suddenly.

"Meredith Fields?" asked the brunette woman in uniform. She had a nice smile on her face, and she held an iPad in her hands.

Meredith looked up. "Yes?".

"I think you should see this before you fly across the ocean," the flight attendant said, turning the screen of the iPad to face Meredith..

"What are you doing?" Lily said. "She's not supposed to "

Lily's protests were left hanging in the air when a video on the iPad started playing. It was a recording of Elijah's TV appearance, confessing his feelings, saying that he was willing to give up being president just to be with her.

The tears she was trying to swallow flowed freely down her cheeks. She raised her head and looked at the smiling cabin crew, who were clearly delighted and giddy.

Meredith bit her lip and took a quick glance at Lily who was frozen, still looking at the iPad.

"Do you think… it's too late for me to get off the plane?" she asked the flight attendant.

The woman smiled then shook her head.

Meredith looked at Lily who was already on her feet, looking more energetic than ever.

"Well, what are you waiting for? I think there's a man you need to track down."

Lily made it sound like a manhunt. Yes, she was out to hunt down the man who had stolen her heart.

Dropping the magazine, she grabbed Lily's wrist and they ran down the aisle of the plane together.

She was in pursuit of her happiness.

And it was to be with Elijah.

$\mathcal{E}$li paced back and forth in his office at campaign headquarters with his arms crossed over his chest as he watched the election coverage. He grew more and more anxious with every passing minute. He hadn't even bothered to try and look good. He hadn't shaved, but at least he'd taken a quick shower this morning. He just felt like there wasn't any need to make the effort..

He doubted his chances of winning after what he'd done on television.

When the results started rolling in, he was shocked when he saw that people were responding positively to his message of love… or they were voting for him out of pity, one of the two. He didn't know.

The campaign staff and volunteers had gathered in the main room, watching the bank of televisions to monitor the results of voting. He joined them for a couple of minutes then retreated back to his office and ended up staring at the photos lined up behind his desk – one of him and Henry, another of him with Ellie and their mom.

Eli breathed in and out slowly.

Soon he would be surrounded by people. Time to put his slightly-scruffy game face on..

There was only an hour left before people started gathering. And that's when he would really start sweating bullets. Though he had already stated that he was willing to give up the presidency, he couldn't help but feel weary.

He had worked so hard for it, after all.

His eyes traveled to the door of the headquarters, wondering if Meredith even saw the broadcast – silently hoping that she would magically appear in front of him somehow.

It'd been hours since the broadcast. It was all over the news and social media sites. How could she have missed it? She had been out of touch since the scandal broke out. And he had been waiting for her call. If she would just call him…

God, he missed hearing her angelic voice.

But of course, if their positions were reversed, he would have fled the country by now.

Is that what she did?

The mere idea of being miles apart from Meredith made his heart sink. He sat on his swivel chair and rested his head in his hands, leaning over. He closed his eyes, trying to enjoy the peacefulness of his office. Hopefully people would stop bombarding him with questions now that the election was almost over.

When he heard the tapping of heels on the floor, he opened his eyes immediately… it was just Sosie. He looked at her without hiding his disappointment, then turned away.

After his confession on air, Sosie had turned ice cold. She was extremely displeased with what he'd done. And he was almost certain that she'd been the one who leaked the affair to the press.

He turned away from the door to face a TV screen which silently replayed a clip of him. It was an ad he'd made for the campaign. The image was replaced with several people clustered around a table, talking about their take on what he'd said.

He sighed, feeling suffocated and claustrophobic even though he was alone in his office.

His fingers rested on the handset of his office phone impatiently. He had considered calling Meredith a million times. But no… his pride was stopping him.

He had made a heartfelt plea on national TV. And calling her from a landline just to get around Sosie who had his mobile phone would be dumb.

He was desperate, yes. But he hadn't considered begging – not yet.

Because if Meredith felt the same way, she would come back to him.

And he was blindly hoping that she would…

He groaned in frustration, putting his head on the table. He was so damn tired, but couldn't rest. Everything was just getting more and more intense and complicated.

And a nap was a luxury he couldn't afford, not yet.

He closed his eyes, hoping that when he opened them again, things would be a little better.

"Hey…" said a familiar voice. His eyes snapped open.

He straightened up in his seat to make sure he wasn't dreaming.

Before him was Meredith, looking at him with her deep blue eyes. She was panting heavily like she had just finished a marathon. There was an uncertain smile on her lips as she walked toward his desk hesitantly.

Elijah blinked, getting up from his seat, meeting her halfway. Tears formed in his eyes as he looked over her beautiful face. His heart skipped a beat when she reached out to touch his face.

"You… you're here," he murmured softly, putting his hands on either side of her face, feeling the warmth of her touch – making sure she was relaxed.

Meredith nodded as tears rolled down her cheeks.

"I'm here," she spoke softly, her breath touching his face.

"I –"

"Shh…" she shushed him, putting a finger on his mouth. She smiled at him, wiping away the tears that had escaped his eyes. "I'm sorry for doubting you."

"No. I'm sorry for being a coward," he muttered, grinning back at her.

He pulled her in for a tight hug, soothing them both after missing out on each other for the past few weeks. Having her back in his arms had brought so much happiness to him, he couldn't stop tearing up.

So, this is what it means to love..

When Meredith looked up at him, he leaned his head lower and gently brushed his lips on hers before planting a kiss on her temple.

"I love you, Meredith Fields, my princess," he whispered.

He didn't understand why, but it felt like a thorn had been removed from his heart when he said those words. He felt lighter because finally, he was able to be honest with her.

He'd finally told her the words he had always wanted to say.

She nodded, then smiled.

"I know. I love you too, Mr. Scott. Or should I say, Mr. President?"

The presidency was the furthest thing from his mind. "You realize that I'm going to hold you forever?" He pulled her closer to his body, their chests pressed against each other.

"Forever?" she leaned her head on his muscled chest, inhaling his scent.

"Forever," he smirked as he leaned down to nuzzle her neck.

"Sounds good to me," she responded with a grin.He smelled her hair and kissed her. He devoured her mouth then moved down, latching on her neck, kissing and nibbling on the smooth column of flesh that he missed so badly.

Who would have ever thought that the woman he met at a masquerade sex party, who'd haunted his dreams for weeks would be Meredith?

He'd never expected to meet her again. He hadn't meant to grow attracted to her. And it hadn't been part of his plan to fall in love with her.

But now he had her – for good.

When they broke the kiss, Meredith held his hand and led him to sit back on his chair. She then sat on his lap, teasing him as she rubbed her ass against his throbbing cock.

He groaned.

"Let's watch and wait for the results," she said giggling.

"I have a better idea…" he murmured against her neck, feeling like the luckiest man in the world.

As she continued to torment him mercilessly, he reflected. He really was lucky. Whether he won the election or not, he was with the woman he loved. He was never letting Meredith go again, not this time.

He just needed to get past tonight, and then he could put a ring on her finger. Then a little piece of him would be with her everywhere — just as it should be, he thought.

Wedding bells might just be in the White House's future.

41

Thank you for reading His Virgin! There's a little bit more of Elijah and Meredith, just waiting for you! Get this bonus story FREE — right now — when you sign up for Vivian's mailing list! Head to https://bookhip. com/SFBHHA_for more info.

~

I know that if you liked this, you'll love THE ROYAL REBEL... It's the story of Stellan and Margot. It is set in the glamorous world of the Dirty Royals... and it's FREE right now.

Heavy is the head that wears the crown.

I'm handsome, obscenely wealthy, and straight-laced. Duty and honor come before what I want. I already have a list of wealthy, beautiful girls that are ready to marry me. When I meet pretty, pink haired, punk-rock Margot, I make myself a deal. I can take her... but only for one earth shattering night.

Proud, rebellious, a perfect body made for sin. Margot is my weakness; it's too bad that she's also a journalist. When she shows up again in Copenhagen, she is tasked with doing a story about me and the future of the royal line.

And me? I can look at Margot all I want... but never ever touch her. So instead I throw up my walls, insisting that our night together was a mistake. It sparks a fire, a growing tension between us.

Every time our hands brush, every single lustful glance, every damn time she bites her lip... Eventually, even my strong will can't overcome temptation. Though it's wrong, though my life is already all plotted out, I can't resist her.

I *need* her, in my bed and in my life.

It's inevitable. The only question is, once I give in and take what I need... will having Margot just one more time be enough?

Start the story of Stellan and Margot right now for FREE with The Royal Rebel.

ABOUT VIVIAN WOOD

Vivian likes to write about troubled, deeply flawed alpha males and the fiery, kick-ass women who bring them to their knees.

Vivian's lasting motto in romance is a quote from a favorite song: "Soulmates never die."

Be sure to join her email list to keep up with all the awesome giveaways, author videos, ARC opportunities, and more!

Vivian's Works

Married At Midnight Series
Forbidden Billionaire Romance
Deal With The Devil
Wed to the Devil

Vow to the he Devil

Ruined castle series
Forbidden Billionaire Romance
The Scottish Billionaire
The Beast
The nanny
The caress

Broken Slipper series
Forbidden Billionaire Romance
The Patron
The Dancer
The Embrace
Possessive

Ravaged Dream Series - coming 2023
Forbidden Billionaire Romance
Grumpy Billionaire Boss
Sweetly Forbidden Intern
Dirty Workplace Secret

Dirty royals
Forbidden Royal Romance
The Royal Rebel
The Wicked Prince
His Forbidden Princess
Royal Fake Fiancé

Lyon Dynasty world
Dark Billionaire Romance
King's Capture
Queen's Sacrifice

SINFULLY RICH SERIES
Steamy Billionaire Romance
SINFUL FLING
SINFUL ENEMY
SINFUL BOSS
SINFUL CHANCE
SINFULLY RICH

HIS AND HERS SERIES
HIS BEST FRIEND'S LITTLE SISTER
CLAIMING HER INNOCENCE
HIS TO KEEP
HIS VIRGIN

THE ADDICTION DUET
ADDICTION
OBSESSION

OTHER BOOKS
WILD HEARTS

For more information….
vivian-wood.com
info@vivian-wood.com

www.ingramcontent.com/pod-product-compliance
Lightning Source LLC
Chambersburg PA
CBHW061152210726
48294CB00006B/1650